Dear Reader,

I can hardly believe that it is almost twenty years since I wrote my first Harlequin book. The thrill of having that book accepted and then seeing it on the bookshelves—being picked up and chosen by readers—is one I shall never forget.

Twenty years seems a long time. So much has happened during those years; so much has changed and yet so much remains the same. The changes that we have all seen within society are, I believe, reflected in the books we, as Harlequin authors, write. They mirror the changes that take place around us in our own and our readers' lives. Our heroines have changed, matured, grown up, as indeed I have done myself. I cannot tell you how much pleasure it gives me to be able to write of mature—as well as young—women finding love. And, of course, love is something that has not changed. Love is still love and always will be, because love is, after all, an intrinsic, vital component of human happiness.

As I read through these books that are being reissued in this Collector's Edition, they bring back for me many happy memories of the times when I wrote them, and I hope that my readers, too, will enjoy the same nostalgia and pleasure.

I wish you all very many hours of happy reading and lives blessed with love.

Penny Jordan

Back by Popular Demand

Penny Jordan is one of the world's best loved as well as bestselling authors, and she was first published by Harlequin in 1981. The novel that launched her career was *Falcon's Prey*, and since then she has gone on to write more than one hundred books. In this special collection, Harlequin is proud to bring back a selection of these highly sought after novels. With beautiful cover art created by artist Erica Just, this is a Collector's Edition to cherish.

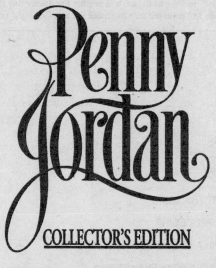

Penny Jordan

COLLECTOR'S EDITION

Unspoken Desire

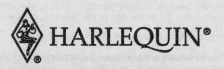

HARLEQUIN®

TORONTO • NEW YORK • LONDON
AMSTERDAM • PARIS • SYDNEY • HAMBURG
STOCKHOLM • ATHENS • TOKYO • MILAN • MADRID
PRAGUE • WARSAW • BUDAPEST • AUCKLAND

ISBN 0-373-63063-8

UNSPOKEN DESIRE

First North American Publication 1991.

Copyright © 1990 by Penny Jordan.

This edition published by arrangement with Harlequin Books S.A.

® and TM are trademarks of the publisher. Trademarks indicated with
® are registered in the United States Patent and Trademark Office, the
Canadian Trade Marks Office and in other countries.

Visit us at www.romance.net

Printed in U.S.A.

ERICA JUST
cover illustrator for the
Penny Jordan Collector's Edition

Erica Just is an artist and illustrator working in various media, including watercolor, pen and ink, and textiles. Her studio is in Nottingham, England.

Her work is inspired by the natural forms, architecture and vibrant colors that she has experienced on her travels, most especially in Africa and India.

Erica has exhibited her work extensively in Great Britain and Europe and has works in private and public collections. As an illustrator she works for a number of companies and also lectures on textile design throughout the country.

CHAPTER ONE

'REBECCA my dear…such a relief! For one moment when you didn't answer the phone straight away I thought perhaps you'd decided to fly out to Australia to see your parents and brother. How *is* dear Robert, by the way, and Ailsa and the girls? They must be getting quite big now. How old are they? Four and two, isn't it? It's…'

'Aunt Maud,' Rebecca interrupted firmly, tucking the receiver under her chin, and trying to concentrate on the essays she was marking while at the same time following the convoluted drift of her great-aunt's vague conversation.

'Ah, yes… The reason I'm ringing you, my dear, is that I desperately need your help.'

Her help? Rebecca's frown wasn't caused entirely by the essay of a pupil who was destined to follow his father into the latter's merchant bank, and yet at ten years old still seemed to think the word instalment possessed a double 'l'.

'*My* help?' She couldn't resist the faintly ironic underlining of the possessive pronoun. At the other end of the line in faraway Cumbria there was the kind of humming silence that told her that her point had been made.

'Well, my dear, there was simply no one else I could turn to,' came the dramatic response. Aunt Maud at her thespian best, Rebecca reflected ruefully, catching the note of pathos that had been added to her great-aunt's original vagueness. 'I would have got in touch with your mother, but since she's in Australia…'

A slight suspicion of aggrieved irritation there, Rebecca suspected, and no wonder. She could well imagine that, whatever kind of help it was she needed, Maud Aysgarth would rather have approached her soft-hearted and far too put-upon mother than herself.

Her mind was more on her marking than her aunt's conversation. Those people who believed that schoolteachers did nothing during the long school holidays really ought to see her desk right now, loaded down as it was, not only with the end-of-term essays from the pupils she taught at an exclusive co-educational private prep school, but also the uncompleted work schedules and plans for the coming autumn and winter terms, she reflected grimly. She loved teaching and always had, and counted herself privileged to have a job teaching in a school as well equipped and well run as the one she did…a private London prep school whose pupils were on the whole well-behaved and keen to learn.

Thinking of her work caused her to lose the thread of her aunt's conversation; after all, what could there possibly be to worry about at Aysgarth with Frazer in charge?

Aysgarth was Frazer's private kingdom, a kingdom in which nothing was allowed to go wrong, nothing allowed to intrude which Frazer did not want intruding, as she knew to her cost.

Aysgarth was a granite-hard house owned by a granite-hard man. And yet she loved the house, and once she had thought…

'So you see, my dear, with Frazer away and myself in charge, there was really no one else I could turn to. I don't know how long it will take you to get up here, but…'

Get up there? Had Aunt Maud gone mad or had she? She must know quite well that if Frazer hadn't actually forbidden Rebecca to put as much as a fingertip on Aysgarth property, then he had certainly made it quite plain that her presence was not one he wanted or welcomed, and why. Rebecca laughed mirthlessly and soundlessly to herself. Why? Because once she had been idiotic enough to want to protect *him* from hurt. For that she had been condemned and ostracised, made to feel as though she were a Judas and worse.

Dear God, the last thing she needed right now was to start walking down that painful path again. It was over, in the past...totally without relevance to her life. A good life—a life filled with a job she enjoyed, friends who shared her interests and tastes, men who took her out, flattered her, flirted with her and, above all, did not look at her with cold grey eyes, the colour of ice, so dark with contempt and bitterness that they shrivelled her very soul.

She was happy, content; her life was rich and full. There was no room in it for useless daydreams, for might-have-beens. She was twenty-six years old, mature, well adjusted, self-sufficient.

Or she had been until Great-Aunt Maud had started interfering in her life, reminding her of things best forgotten. And then something her aunt had said hit her.

'Frazer isn't at Aysgarth? But he must be! Rory and Lillian left the children there because...'

'That's just what I'm trying to tell you, my dear. Frazer *was* here, but at the very last minute he had to take over from one of his colleagues, who was due to give a lecture tour in the States. Frazer had no option but to go in his place, as Head of the Institute. He'll be gone for nearly three months.'

'Three months?' Rebecca was appalled. 'What

about the children?' From what her mother had told her, Frazer's niece and nephew, his brother's children, were a pretty unruly pair, who required a very firm hand on the reins. Eight-year-old twins whose easygoing father had never made any real attempt to discipline them, and who with their mother had calmly dumped them on Frazer eight months ago, so that he could take up a new job in Hong Kong.

'Well, Frazer did make proper arrangements for them,' Aunt Maud was saying defensively. She had always hated anyone criticising Frazer. After his and Rory's parents had been killed in an air crash she had moved into Aysgarth House at Frazer's request. He had been eighteen then and Rory a much younger twelve. 'He hired a young woman to take charge of them.'

A sniff accompanied the almost scathing words 'a young woman', and Rebecca, who had heard all about the twins' exploits from her mother who regularly kept in touch with Frazer, her much younger cousin, repressed a faint sigh of sympathy for the girl concerned.

'What's happened to her?' Rebecca asked drily.

'She's left—handed in her notice and said that there was no way she was going to be responsible for the twins. Undisciplined brats, was how she referred to them.'

In her mind's eye, Rebecca pictured her great-aunt's magnificently Edwardian bosom heaving in righteous indignation at this slur on the Aysgarth line, but she was long past being intimidated by the long shadow that name had once cast across her life—a long, long time ago when she had been awed and impressed by the stories her mother had told her about her ancestors' long-ago deeds of valour.

Holidays spent at Aysgarth had not helped to dispel the awe—not with Frazer there, ten years her senior. Darkly if rather grimly handsome even in those days, a silent spectator of hers and Rory's games, a dark-visaged god who had walked casually into her life and her heart.

'Well, aren't they?' she said wryly now, groaningly dismissing her own ridiculous vulnerabilities.

There was a moment's silence and then her great-aunt admitted with obvious difficulty, 'Perhaps they *are* a little high-spirited, but at their age...'

'They're out of control,' Rebecca interrupted crisply, 'and I suspect that one of the reasons Rory has dumped them on Frazer is that he hopes that Frazer will apply some of that famous discipline of his on them. What they really need is to go to a good school where their energies and high spirits will be channelled properly.'

'Exactly!' Maud pounced eagerly. 'That's just why I'm ringing you...with your teaching experience.' Much, much too late Rebecca saw the trap closing fast around her. 'Of course, if your dear mother were here... However, I remember how much you enjoyed staying at Aysgarth as a child...all those long summer holidays...'

Rebecca silently and grimly acknowledged the application of a generous amount of emotional pressure to her aunt's argument. Without actually putting it into so many words, her aunt was implying that it was her duty to drop everything and go haring off to Cumbria in order to take charge of Rory's twins...that she owed it to the family to do so.

A dozen good reasons why she ought to refuse came readily and easily to mind; not the least of them the fact that she had already made tentative plans to spend at least part of her summer break touring Greece with some friends, but even as the words formed she found herself being relentlessly and determinedly dragged into her great-aunt's carefully woven net.

She made one last bid for freedom, saying desperately, 'Aunt Maud, you know that Frazer won't like it!'

There was a telling silence and then her aunt's voice, vague and faintly ominously tired, saying plaintively, 'Oh, dear...but, Rebecca, that was all so long ago. I'm sure Frazer has forgotten all about it. He never was one to hold a grudge…such a silly quarrel anyway.'

Silly or not, it had been important enough to keep her away from Aysgarth for the eight years, and to keep Frazer from inviting her there.

They had met twice in all that time; once briefly at the twins' christening…an appearance which pride alone had demanded she put in when, as she remembered all too well, Frazer had treated her with grim and very determined silence, as though she had physically ceased to exist.

The second occasion had been when her brother Robert and Ailsa had got married. She had been bridesmaid, Rory's two toddlers attendants along with some of Ailsa's cousins, and in the hurly-burly of looking after half a dozen assorted children, she had managed to avoid any kind of direct confrontation with Frazer very nicely indeed.

To have her presence requested, almost demanded, in fact, at Aysgarth after all this time was the last thing she had expected.

If Frazer had been there it would have been impossible for her to go…not because of his dislike of her, but for the sake of her own pride, but of course, he wasn't there. If he had been there the problem wouldn't have arisen in the first place; but the problem *had* arisen, and despite all her doubts, all the reasons why she ought firmly but pleasantly to refuse to go to her great-aunt's aid, she knew that she couldn't do it.

Illogical, ridiculous it might be, but there was a debt she owed, if not to Frazer himself, then at least to Maud, who had made both her and Robert so very welcome in the days when her father's career had meant that he and their mother were so often out of the country.

Now it was her turn to repay that kindness…and repay it she must, if only to prove that whatever Frazer might think, it was by her *own* decision that she stayed away from Aysgarth, and not because of any stipulation of his.

Not that he had ever verbally announced that she was not to return; the veto had been more subtle than that, and more hurtful. And it *had* been there, no matter how much Aunt Maud might try to gloss over it now.

Knowing she was probably going to regret it, she gave in, but warned, 'It will be the end of the week before I can get up there.'

IT WAS ONLY after she had replaced the receiver that Rebecca wondered what on earth she had committed herself to. Virtually three full months looking after two thoroughly undisciplined children, in a house whose owner both disliked and despised her.

Her flatmate was astounded when she told her what she had agreed to do.

'But you had so much planned!' she expostulated. 'The trip to Greece, and...'

'I know, but it *is* an emergency and I felt obliged to help out. A family emergency.'

Kate Summerfield frowned at her. 'You've never mentioned having family in Cumbria before—and I don't recall you ever going to see them.'

The two girls had shared a flat since leaving university, and when Rebecca had announced four years previously that she intended to buy her own small property Kate had readily agreed to become her lodger.

'For a very good reason,' Rebecca told her wryly, and proceeded to explain.

'You mean he actually banned you from visiting the house? What on earth had you done?'

Rebecca shook her head.

'It wasn't as obvious as that. There was no direct ban as such. It was far more subtle than that...just the intimation that my presence was no longer welcome.'

'Why? What had you done? Pawned the family jewels or something?' Kate joked.

'Not exactly.' Rebecca bit her lip. She had never discussed the reason for Frazer's ban with anyone, not even her parents, who, like Maud, presumed that they had quarrelled about something far less serious.

'It's rather a long story,' she said slowly, groping for the right words, suddenly almost desperately wanting to unburden herself to someone. Her conversation with Maud had resurrected old hurts, opened old wounds, and the need to share them with someone overpowered her normal reticence on the subject.

Kate looked speculatively at her and said, 'I've got plenty of time. Come on, tell me all about it.'

'Well, it was just after my eighteenth birthday. My parents were away at the time out in South America. I was going to spend the summer holiday at Aysgarth as usual. Rory came to collect me from school. He wanted to show off his new car. He'd been married about six months then, and Lillian was expecting the twins.

'Frazer hadn't wanted him to get married. He thought he was too young at twenty-one to make such a commitment, but Rory overruled him. I could tell the moment he picked me up that something was wrong—we'd always got on very well together.'

'Just like brother and sister?' Kate interposed questioningly.

Rebecca returned her look and said truthfully, 'Exactly like brother and sister. I asked him what was wrong and on the way home he told me. He'd been having an affair and Frazer had found out. They'd been seen together and somehow or other Frazer had got to know about it. Frazer was demanding to know who it was that he was involved with.'

'And?' probed Kate as Rebecca's voice slowed down.

'And Rory didn't want to tell him. You see, the woman he'd been involved with was actually Frazer's girlfriend. She and her family had only recently moved to the area and Rory seemed to think that Frazer was pretty keen on her.'

'And?' Kate probed again.

Rebecca shrugged her shoulders tiredly. 'It's all very simple really. Rory asked me if I'd let him tell Frazer that it had been me he'd been involved with.' She gave a faint sigh. 'I suppose it was naïve of me, but when Rory said how much Frazer loved Michelle and how much it would hurt him if he found out that she and Rory had been having an affair—well, I...'

'You were eighteen years old, desperately in love and only too anxious to do anything you could to save the object of that love from pain,' Kate hazarded wryly.

Rebecca laughed a little sadly. 'Was I so very obvious?' she questioned.

Her friend shook her head. 'It all fits. I take it you *were* in love with this Frazer.'

'I certainly thought I was,' Rebecca agreed drily, 'although, in the light of the events that followed, that love very quickly turned to hatred. It was never any more than a teenage crush really,' she added dismissively.

It had rather jolted her that Kate had so easily recognised her true feelings, and she wondered how many other people at the time had known exactly how she'd felt about Frazer. She had certainly done very little to hide her adoration of him.

'Are you trying to tell me that this Frazer actually believed you were having an affair with Rory?' Kate asked in some astonishment.

Rebecca frowned. 'Well, yes. Well, yes, he did. He was furious about it, of course—accused me of trying to break up Rory's marriage, pointed out that Rory's wife was expecting, said all the usual sort of things one might expect.'

'And he really genuinely had no idea that you were making it up?'

'No,' Rebecca told her blankly. 'Why?'

Kate shrugged and said drily, 'Well, no reason. He seems a bit of an idiot, though—first of all he doesn't realise the girl he's in love with is having an affair with his brother and then he believes that the girl who loves him *is* having an affair with his brother. A bit dense, is he?' she questioned.

Rebecca's frown deepened. 'No, he isn't. In fact if anything he's extremely perceptive—too perceptive sometimes.'

Kate said nothing, but the look she gave her friend said it all for her.

'He would have wanted to believe me,' Rebecca told her defensively, without even knowing why she should want to defend Frazer. He certainly didn't deserve it, nor need it, not when she remembered the tongue-lashing he had given her when Rory had confessed to him that it was she with whom he had been involved.

'You mean it was preferable to believe that *you* were guilty of enticing his brother into an extra-marital relationship rather than his girlfriend?' Kate demanded scathingly. 'That isn't perception, Rebecca, it's sheer bloody-minded stupidity. What happened?' she asked offhandedly. 'About his relationship with the girlfriend, I mean.'

Rebecca frowned again. 'That's the odd thing about it all, really. It just sort of petered out. Well, at least that's the impression that the rest of the family seemed to have. I suppose pride kept Frazer from admitting the truth to anyone, that he'd loved her and lost her.'

'Mmm,' Kate commented absently. She appeared

to be concentrating on a small speck of fluff on the carpet. 'And the two of you kept your distance from one another ever since, is that it?'

Rebecca shrugged. 'Frazer made it plain to me that my presence wouldn't be welcome at Aysgarth in the future. Nothing he's ever said or done has contradicted that impression.'

'And now you're being summoned up to Cumbria to look after his brother's brats in his absence,' Kate supplied wryly. 'Well, I wonder what he's going to say when he finds out about that.'

'Do you think perhaps I oughtn't to go?' Rebecca asked anxiously.

Despite her stunning good looks and her undoubted intelligence, not to mention her skill with her pupils, Rebecca had a sometimes disconcerting lack of self-worth, something which had always puzzled Kate, but which she now suspected she knew the reason for.

'On the contrary,' Kate told her firmly. 'I think you ought to go,' and then, as she saw relief lighten her friend's features, she added softly, 'I suppose it never occurred to you that you could tell him the truth?' She watched as the colour left Rebecca's face and added, as though unaware of it, 'After all, there's no reason why you shouldn't now, is there? As you said yourself, the relationship with the girl in question petered out. Why haven't you told him, Rebecca?' she pressed.

Rebecca turned her back on her, fidgeting with some papers on her desk.

'Why should I? There's no reason to. If he wants to believe the worst of me, then let him.'

'Well, it certainly provides a very effective barrier to hide behind,' said Kate obliquely, watching in compassion as the telltale colour ran up under her friend's fair skin. It was an unusual combination, that blonde, silky fall of hair and that pale Celtic skin. Unusual and very, very attractive.

Kate had lost count of the number of men she had introduced to her flatmate, who had promptly all fallen head over heels with her air of fragile, almost haunted vulnerability. As far as she knew, Rebecca had never even come close to returning their feelings. She had often wondered why her friend appeared so immune to the male sex. Now she suspected she had found the answer.

'I can't do it,' Rebecca suddenly burst out despairingly. 'I can't go up there!'

'Don't be ridiculous,' Kate told her dampeningly. 'Of course you can, and so you should. You've already told your aunt you will. It would be unfair to let her down. What are you frightened of, Rebecca?' she probed gently. 'Even if this Frazer should return home early and find you there, he's hardly going to physically throw you out, is he? I think in your shoes,' she mused thoughtfully, 'I should rather enjoy the opportunity to make him indebted to me.'

Rebecca gave her a despairing look. She didn't know Frazer. She had no idea that Frazer of all people was the very last person to relish being indebted to anyone, and especially to her.

'But then, of course, he's already indebted to you, isn't he?' Kate added almost as though she had read the course of her thoughts, and when Rebecca stared at her she added softly, 'You sacrificed your good name and feelings to protect that of his girl-friend and his feelings,' she pointed out wryly. 'You're not frightened of him, are you, Rebecca?' she asked curiously, knowing full well the effect her question would have.

'Of course I'm not,' Rebecca denied robustly.

'Good. Then there's nothing to stop you fulfilling your promise to your aunt, is there?'

For a moment Rebecca was silent, then she agreed hollowly, 'No. Nothing at all.'

CHAPTER TWO

KNOWING that and actually believing it were two very different things, as Rebecca quickly discovered as she made her preparations to leave for Cumbria. Instead of worrying about Frazer and his all too likely reaction to the discovery that she was installed in his home, it would be far more profitable for her to spend her time worrying about how she was going to control the twins, she reflected as she packed her small car for the journey north.

The class of ten-year-olds she taught were in the main intelligent and well-disciplined children. All the reports she had heard of Rory's twins suggested that, although they might possess intelligence, they certainly did not possess any self-discipline, and by all accounts resented any attempt to impose it on them. Remembering her own and Robert's feelings when their parents had to constantly go away without them, Rebecca wondered privately if their unruliness did not perhaps spring more from a desire to capture parental attention rather than from any inborn disruptiveness.

Great-Aunt Maud possessed not only an Edwardian bosom, but in addition an Edwardian attitude to
life, and at her behest Rebecca had promised that
she would try to be at Aysgarth for four o'clock in
time for afternoon tea.

'That will give you an ideal opportunity in which
to meet the children,' Aunt Maud had informed her,
and Rebecca, suddenly remembering from her own
childhood her great-aunt's ability on occasions to
put aside her vagueness and apparent fragility and
reveal all the assets of a master tactician, wondered
a little uneasily why it was that Maud required her
assistance in managing the twins. After all, as she
remembered very well, Great-Aunt Maud had had
no difficulty at all in keeping both her and Robert
under control.

That had been almost twenty years ago, though,
when her aunt had been in her fifties. Now she was
in her seventies, and it was hardly to be expected
that she could keep a watchful eye on two energetic
and by all accounts extremely difficult eight-year-
olds.

Aysgarth was on the more distant side of Cumbria, far away from the popular Lake District, in
what Rory had on more than one occasion discon-
solately described as the back of beyond.

Rebecca, despite the fact that she had lived and
worked in London for well over six years, did not

share his views. In London she had a lifestyle she enjoyed and a job she loved, but, given freedom of choice, she knew that she could quite easily adapt to a more rural lifestyle.

It surprised her to see how far the motorway system had now penetrated into Cumbria, giving her the advantage of gaining a good half-hour on her estimated journey time. With that half-hour in mind, a couple of miles away from Aysgarth and halfway down a very narrow country lane that led not only to the house but to the several farms beyond it, she pulled her car in to the side of the road and got out, locking it.

Fifty yards or so down into the valley lay one of the favourite spots of her childhood and teenage years. The river ran through the valley, dammed at one end to form a small pool from which it spilled over a weir, dropping quite a formidable distance into the far end of the valley and beyond that the valley below it.

The valley was wooded, shadowy with trees and their secrets. Underfoot the ground was springy and resinous with pine needles and roots. Despite the fact that the weather forecasters had promised them a good summer, so far there had been very little evidence of it, and as Rebecca made her way down the steep-sided valley she saw that the river below was flooded from the heavy spring rains.

Down below her in the valley bottom, a movement caught her attention. She focused on it abruptly, frowning as she saw the two small jean-clad figures hurrying in the direction of Aysgarth House. The twins. She would have recognised them through their similarity to their dark-haired and dark-visaged uncle anywhere, and she mused ruefully on the oddity of heredity and the fact that it should be Rory's children who had inherited so much of Frazer's dark colouring. Rory himself took after his and Frazer's mother, being fair-haired and blue-eyed, whereas Frazer took after their father, possessing the dark-haired, grey-eyed, hard-chiselled look which had always been formidably recognisable as Aysgarth features.

It was not their similarity to their uncle that brought a frown to Rebecca's forehead, though; it was the fact that the two children, barely eight years old, were apparently free to wander the countryside at will. She could remember herself how very strict not only Aunt Maud but also Frazer himself had been about her liking to wander here in this remote and beautiful valley. How he had drummed into her the danger of going too near the weir, or being tempted to even think about swimming in the pool, which was extremely deep and possessed dangerous hidden currents.

It was true that the twins had not been swimming, but she seemed to remember she had been well into her teens before Frazer had lifted the ban that stipulated that she was never ever allowed to come down here on her own.

As the twins approached, some instinct made her draw back into the shadow of the enclosing trees. The path they were on ran several yards away from her, and as she knew, turned abruptly several yards away to veer in the direction of Aysgarth House. As they passed her she could hear Peter saying anxiously to his sister. 'Are you sure it'll work, Helen? Are you sure it'll make her go away?'

Rebecca stiffened, knowing instinctively that they were discussing her own arrival.

Frowning fiercely, Helen Aysgarth was a minute replica of her formidable uncle.

'Maybe not at first,' she allowed judiciously, 'but it won't take long.'

'Why did Aunt Maud have to send for her anyway?' Peter muttered bitterly. 'A schoolteacher! As if we didn't have enough of schoolteachers when we're at school!'

'We'll soon get rid of her,' Helen comforted her twin. 'After all, we got rid of Carole, didn't we?'

Both of them giggled and Peter added victoriously, 'And Jane. Uncle Frazer was really angry when we told him Jane wanted to marry him, wasn't he?'

'Furious,' Helen agreed with obvious enjoyment.

With every word she overheard, Rebecca's heart sank further. What on earth was she letting herself in for, and why?

'Norty says Cousin Becky will soon teach us to mind our manners,' Peter reminded his sister.

Helen said witheringly, 'Cousin Becky! We've never even met her, have we, apart from that once at the wedding, and I bet she isn't coming here because of us at all. I bet it's because of Frazer. Norty says he's the best catch in the area and it's high time he settled down and had some children of his own.'

Furious, exasperated and conscious of a growing numbness in her cramped limbs, Rebecca stayed where she was.

Norty—Mrs Norton—was Frazer's housekeeper. She had been with the family during Frazer and Rory's parents' lifetime, and Rebecca remembered her with particular fondness. She hoped it wasn't from the housekeeper that the twins had got the idea that she had come up here solely on account of Frazer, and as for *that* idea—well, she decided grimly, she would very quickly disabuse them of it!

She wasn't a shy eighteen-year-old any more. What she had once felt for Frazer had long ago died—perhaps a little more violently and cruelly than it would have done in the normal course of events, but its death had been a necessary one. Most girls went through a period of intense emotional adulation for some older man. Most of them, though, were far too sensible to fix that adulation on a member of their own family.

She had thought of Frazer as some kind of Olympian being, all-knowing, all-wise, all-seeing. No virtue had been too high for him to reach. What a fool she had been when, desperate and trapped, Rory had begged her to help him, she had done so willingly, delighting in the opportunity to sacrifice herself for the greater good. Frazer's greater good.

If she had expected that somehow or other he would divine the truth, she had been bitterly disappointed. If she had expected that he would not only divine the truth, but lavish praise and gratitude on her for that sacrifice, she had been doubly disappointed. What he had in actual fact done was to read her such a savage and bitter lecture that it had been months if not years before she had ever been able to hold up her head again.

At first shock had numbed the worst of her feelings of degradation and humiliation, but then, as the shock wore off, reality had begun to take its place; the reality of realising that Frazer condemned her for what he had termed as her criminal and idiotic folly in becoming involved in an affair with his brother.

If once she had hoped he would come to see the truth, now she no longer did. Now she doubted that it would make any difference even if he did know the truth. Frazer had never liked being wrong about anything, she remembered bitterly.

The children were walking past her now, and just as they started to move out of sight she heard Peter saying anxiously, 'You don't think she'll see the glass and stop, do you?' and her heart somersaulted in sudden shock and outrage as she heard Helen telling him matter-of-factly,

'She can't, not where we put it.'

'Do you think she'll know we've done it?' Peter demanded. 'Do you think she'll tell Aunt Maud?'

'No,' Helen assured him, 'but later on, when she realises that we intend to make her leave, then she'll know we did it,' she added with relish.

'But she isn't like the others,' Peter told his sister. 'She's our cousin.'

'Our second cousin,' Helen contradicted flatly. 'And you know what'll happen if she stays. She'll just be like all the others, mooning about after Uncle Frazer, and then, if he gets interested in her and marries her and they have children of their own, what's going to happen to us?'

All the anger and disbelief Rebecca had been experiencing as she listened to the twins plotting vanished abruptly as she heard the fear and loneliness behind those last words. What was going to happen to them indeed? By all accounts Rory and Lilian's marriage was not a happy one. The reason that Lillian had agreed to accompany Rory on this Hong Kong contract in the first place, according to what Rebecca's mother had confided to her, was that she felt it necessary to keep an eye on her errant husband.

Since the children were not allowed to go with them, it had been necessary to find somebody else to take charge of them. Frazer, of course, had been the natural choice.

Having herself been the child of parents who of necessity had had to spend long periods of time out of the country, her father before he had retired having been a diplomat, Rebecca was very familiar with the attacks of isolation and loneliness that could hit children separated from their parents for long periods of time. That was one of the reasons she made such a good teacher, or so her head had told her. She readily understood the fears and anxieties of those children who actually boarded at the school and seemed to have the knack of being able to soothe and comfort them. However, while she and Robert had had parents who had been absent for long periods during their childhood, they had never for one moment doubted their parents' love and concern for them.

Helen and Peter, it seemed, did, and perhaps with good reason, she acknowledged uneasily. It was no secret in the family that Lillian had been annoyed when she'd discovered that she was pregnant a matter of months after she and Rory were married.

She had been twenty, Rory twenty-two—two spoiled and self-indulgent young people who had married on a whim and conceived the twins without a moment's thought for the future responsibilities they would bring.

Rory had always been lightweight compared with Frazer, eager to taste every one of life's pleasures, self-indulgent to the extreme. Fun to be with if fun was all one wanted from life, but with no substance to fall back on for life's difficult and unhappy times.

'If Frazer gets married, his new wife won't want us living at Aysgarth. Everyone says that,' Helen reminded her brother. 'That means we'll have to go away to boarding school or go and live with Gran and Gramps in Brighton.'

'Perhaps Mum and Dad might come back and Dad will get a job here in England,' Peter suggested hopefully, but Helen quelled his suggestion with a stern frown.

'You know he won't,' she told her brother. 'We heard them arguing about it last Christmas, don't you remember? Mum said she'd leave Dad if it wasn't for us. Anyway, I don't want them to come back, because they're always quarrelling and arguing. I want to stay here at Aysgarth with Frazer.'

Their voices faded as they made their way along the path away from her, and Rebecca felt her heart turn over with pity and compassion for them. Adults forgot how much children saw and heard and felt. Only when she was sure they were safely out of sight and earshot did she make her own way back to her car.

The lane from here to Aysgarth was straight, apart from one particularly bad bend about fifty yards away. Thoughtfully she left her car where it was and walked towards it. As she had suspected, as she rounded the bend, she saw on the road in front of her some dangerously sharp shards of glass which, had she driven over them, must surely have severely damaged if not completely destroyed her tyres.

What neither of the twins could possibly know was that eighteen months before their birth, a very severe accident had been caused on this very bend by broken glass, though not left deliberately in that instance. A bottle which had fallen accidentally from a crate and not been noticed had broken on the road and the young couple in the car had been killed when their tyres had punctured and the car had swerved out of control off the road, plunging down into the valley, where it had burst into flames.

Rebecca was far too sensible and knew far too much about children of the twins' age to imagine for a moment that they had thought far enough ahead to realise the possible outcome of their plans to get rid of her. Death, if they thought about it at all, was to children of that age a concept outside their grasp, unless they were unfortunate enough to suffer the loss of someone close to them.

As she picked up the glass and carefully put it in her handkerchief, carrying it back to the car with her, she pondered on how best to deal with the problem facing her.

All her desire to return to London was now gone. The twins needed her help, even if they themselves did not recognise it.

She got back into her car in a very thoughtful frame of mind indeed. The twins might not be able to recognise their need, but others might. The Great-Aunt Maud she remembered, despite her assumed vagueness and love of drama, had possessed more than her fair share of her nephew's astuteness. Could it be that Maud had summoned her, not so much because she needed help in keeping the twins under control, but because she saw that they needed something more than mere discipline, and perhaps because she was hoping that, given the similarity of their childhood, Rebecca might be able to reach out and give the twins the reassurance and love they so obviously needed.

She was still turning these thoughts over in her mind as she drove in past the gates to Aysgarth. The house had been built by a Victorian Aysgarth who had made his money from the boom in railways and promptly retired to Cumbria with his wife and family.

It was a large, square building, more sturdy than elegant, three storeys high with deep, ample cellars. The sturdy Victorian furniture had been retained by the various generations of Aysgarths to inhabit the house, so that the rooms possessed an air of solid comfort rather than fashionable luxury.

It was a house in which one instantly felt at home, or at least that had always been Rebecca's impression of it as a child. As she drove past the front door to park her car, she saw that the back door was standing open.

Aysgarth was remote enough for its inhabitants not to need to worry about the intentions of any passing caller, and as Rebecca got out of the car she heard a familiar shrill barking and kneeled down just in time to wad off the ecstatic welcome of a spaniel of rather large size and dubious parentage.

The best thing that could probably be said about

Sophy was that she was extremely affectionate, the worst that she was also extremely scatty. As an adult Rebecca had always been rather surprised that Frazer of all people, so meticulous, so hard-edged and determined about everything he did, should actually have given house room to this overexuberant little stray who had wandered into the grounds of Aysgarth House a few weeks before Rebecca's own eighteenth birthday. She had been the one who had found her and who had taken her into the house, bundling her shivering, soaking form in a towel and rubbing her dry till she stopped shivering.

She had pleaded with Norty to be allowed to keep the dog until Frazer came back from the Institute. In those days he had not headed the impressive and very important scientific institute whose work was always shrouded in so much secrecy, but he had still worked hard with very long hours, and it had been almost nine o'clock that evening before he had put her mind at rest and announced that yes, she could keep the stray, providing no one turned up to claim it.

Within twenty-four hours of being in the household, Sophy had firmly and determinedly attached herself to Frazer, becoming not her dog, but Frazer's. However, it seemed she had remembered her, Rebecca reflected as she bent down and scratched behind the long floppy ears.

'Ah, Rebecca! I thought it must be you.' Silver-haired, pink- and white-skinned, dressed always in lavender, cream or black, Great-Aunt Maud, Rebecca had often thought, would surely look far more at home in some genteel establishment in Bournemouth rather than up here in the granite hills of Cumbria.

Indeed she had for a time after being widowed lived in the south of England, but immediately upon Frazer's request to her to come and take charge of the house she had given up that life and had remained at Aysgarth ever since.

'Ten to four—excellent!' she announced approvingly, waiting for Rebecca to join her, 'I've already warned Mrs Norton that you would be here for afternoon tea. The twins are upstairs washing their hands and faces and changing out of those disgusting jeans all children seem to insist on wearing these days. I can't think what the world's coming to. In my day little girls dressed like little girls,' she added disapprovingly, 'not in this ridiculous dual-sex uniform of jeans that everyone seems to favour these days.'

Rebecca, remembering her own mother's gentle remonstrations and explanations when she herself had protested bitterly about the smocked velvet dress Aunt Maud had insisted on buying for her the Christmas she was twelve years old, considering herself far too grown-up for such a childish outfit, repressed a small smile.

'And while I think about it,' Aunt Maud continued, 'that's another thing that will have to be sorted out. Both of them need new clothes. Such a nuisance, that girl Frazer appointed leaving the way she did.'

'Why did she leave?' asked Rebecca quietly, curious to hear what her aunt would say, wondering exactly how much Maud knew about the twins' plans.

The hallway to Aysgarth was large and square with a parquet floor and an impressive carved wooden staircase running up three sides of it. At the rear of the hall was a large stained glass window, depicting various scenes of relevance to the original builder of the house, including one displaying the arms and colours of the railway which had made him his money.

'Oh, I expect it was the usual thing,' snorted Maud, startling Rebecca for a moment until she added in explanation, 'too few young men and not enough to do on her days and evening off. Young girls these days don't know how fortunate they are,' she continued severely. 'In my day, a girl was expected to get married whether she wanted to or not. We didn't have the freedom you do these days. I'm glad to see you haven't rushed into marriage, Re-

becca,' she added approvingly, then rather spoilt the
effect of this phrase by adding musingly, 'How old
are you now? It must be nearly thirty, surely.'

'Twenty-six, actually,' Rebecca told her, feeling
irritated with herself for her own defensive correc-
tion of her aunt's over-estimation of her age.

'Twenty-six—mm… A very sensible age for a
young woman, I've always thought.'

Rebecca wasn't sure if she actually liked being
described as sensible, but she put aside the thought
to examine later, following her aunt into what was
always described as the small sitting-room, although in fact it was a well-proportioned room that
faced south and because of that was a favourite
room for the family's daytime use.

The yellow damask curtains had faded over the
years to a soft appealing primrose. Rory and Frazer's mother had replaced the original covers on the
settees and chairs with new ones in a rich blue
which had now also faded pleasantly. The walls
were hung with straw-coloured silk and a faded
blue and gold rug covered the parquet floor.

The familiar sight of her aunt's embroidery frame
standing to one side of the fireplace took Rebecca
back to her own childhood. She had never actually
seen a piece of embroidery completed by Aunt
Maud, and she had a shrewd suspicion that the old
lady adopted the embroidery as a skilful means of

extricating herself from any duties she didn't wish to perform.

'Mrs Norton will bring tea through in a second. In the meantime, tell me, my dear, how are your parents and Robert and his family?'

'They're very well,' Rebecca told her, describing the exploits of her niece and nephew to her as relayed to her through the medium of her sister-in-law's latest letter.

'Such a pity you couldn't have gone to Australia with your parents,' Aunt Maud commented, then pursed her lips and added thoughtfully, 'although in the circumstances...'

She broke off as Mrs Norton came in, pushing a tea trolley. The housekeeper beamed when she saw Rebecca, who quickly and fondly embraced her, asking her how she was. It was a good five minutes before she left, confirming that she would go upstairs and find out what was delaying the twins.

'So why didn't you go with your parents, my dear?' Aunt Maud pursued as she poured the tea. 'Is there perhaps a young man in London?'

Mischievously Rebecca deliberately pretended not to understand, frowning and looking quite as vague as her aunt as she asked innocently.

'A young man? London is full of young men, Aunt Maud. Which one was it in particular?'

'You know exactly what I mean, Rebecca,' Aunt Maud interrupted her sternly. 'Is there a particular young man in your life whose presence there made you prefer to stay in London rather than to accompany your parents?'

Cautiously Rebecca hesitated, then said lightly, and not altogether untruthfully, 'There isn't one particular young man, Aunt Maud, but I do have several men friends whom I date from time to time.'

'Date?' snorted Aunt Maud. 'What kind of word is that, and you an English teacher as well? These young men—are their intentions towards you serious, or...'

Rebecca couldn't help it—she burst out laughing.

'They're friends, Aunt Maud. People whose company I enjoy.' She broke off as the sitting-room door opened and the twins came in. A complete metamorphosis appeared to have taken place, not only in their clothes but also in their attitude. Nothing could have been more friendly or appealing than the way they both welcomed her, Rebecca acknowledged, and perhaps because of that and because of what she knew she deliberately decided to punish them a little, waiting until Maud had performed the necessary introductions and the twins were settled with their milk and biscuits before opening her handbag and removing the handkerchief as though to blow her nose.

When the shards of glass fell on to the floor, she looked at them in feigned surprise, meanwhile watching the twins' faces. Peter's showed a sharp stab of fear and guilt; Helen's on the other hand remained impassive after one brief lightning look into her own face.

'Rebecca, what on earth...?' Aunt Maud began.

Rebecca quickly apologised, getting down on the floor to remove the glass and saying quickly, 'Good heavens, I'd forgotten about that! I found it on the road. Luckily I'd stopped the car to look at the view—if I hadn't I would have been bound to have run over it, doing heaven alone knows what damage to the car.'

'Glass?' Aunt Maud was frowning heavily. 'How on earth could that have got there?'

Peter shifted uncomfortably in his chair. Helen was made of sterner stuff; although her face had gone pale, she remained resolutely still.

'Oh, I expect some tourists dropped it,' Rebecca said lightly. 'You know how careless they are. They wouldn't have realised the potential danger they were causing—not just to cars, but to animals as well—you know how scatty Sophy is,' she continued mercilessly. 'She could quite easily have run down there and cut her paw.'

She heard Helen gulp quite audibly and suppressed a small stab of remorse. She doubted that the child had even thought of the potential danger to anyone other than her, their victim, but a timely reminder of how easily somebody or something else could have been injured by the glass might not go amiss.

'Well, I don't know. So careless and thoughtless! As you say, it must have been trippers. Nobody local would have done something so stupid,' said Aunt Maud.

'Yes, that's what I thought,' Rebecca said gently, looking directly at the twins as she added, 'It was just as well that I saw it in time.'

'Just as well indeed,' Aunt Maud approved, then, turning to the twins, she announced firmly, 'There will be no more running wild for you two now that Rebecca's here. She's a schoolteacher and she'll know exactly how to keep the pair of you occupied.'

Rebecca's heart sank as she listened to Aunt Maud's admonishment. The very last thing she wanted was to be held up to the children as some kind of disciplinarian and ogre. Neither, however, did she want either of them to think she was going to deliberately court their approval, so she held back the words she had been about to say and instead, pursuing another line of thought, said calmly,

'You said Frazer was going to be away for three months in all. I'm afraid I won't be able to stay

quite as long as that. Two and a half months is the
very most I can spare,' she fibbed, and added, 'I've
promised to go back to school two weeks early to
help with the preparations for the new term.'

She didn't look at the twins as she spoke, but
wondered a little grimly what they would make of
her announcement, telling them as it did that she
had no intention of staying on until Frazer returned.
She hoped her statement had put at rest their concern that she intended to take Frazer away from
them, but instead of reassuring them it seemed to
bring an expression of extreme truculence to
Helen's face as she began sulkily, 'But Frazer...'

'Uncle Frazer, Helen,' Great-Aunt Maud interrupted loftily. 'You're only a little girl and you
must not address an adult by his or her Christian
name. It's not polite.'

'But Frazer said I could,' Helen persisted dog-
gedly, only to be frowned down by a very cold stare
indeed from her great-aunt.

Rebecca, remembering the effect of that haughty
stare, felt sorry for her, but Helen, it seemed, was
made of far tougher material than she had been at
that age, because she simply ignored the look being
turned upon her and, putting down her glass and
plate, got up unceremoniously.

'Peter and I are going out to play.'

Aunt Maud watched them go in grim silence,

then turned to Rebecca and said, 'You see what I mean about their needing discipline, Rebecca? I really am at my wits' end. Frazer says we must be patient with them and take into account the unfortunate circumstances of their home background. He was never in favour of Rory marrying so young; neither for that matter was I.

'I agree that it's very unfortunate that neither of their parents seems to take a proper interest in their off spring, but I feel that Frazer is far too indulgent with them.'

'And I'm supposed to remedy that?' Rebecca asked her gently.

Her aunt had the grace to look a little embarrassed.

'Not remedy it, perhaps,' she allowed with a small smile, 'but maybe alleviate it, just a little.'

She got up with a sigh, suddenly looking every one of her seventy-odd years. She patted Rebecca lightly on the shoulder and said surprisingly, 'You always were a very kind child, Rebecca. Perhaps it's wrong of me to have taken advantage of that kindness, but I really was at my wits' end. I'm no longer physically capable of taking charge of two energetic eight-year-olds.'

There was sadness as well as resignation in her voice, and Rebecca felt an upsurge of her earlier compassion, this time not for the twins but for her aunt as well.

'I'll do what I can,' she promised her. 'But it isn't going to be easy.'

CHAPTER THREE

IT CERTAINLY wasn't. Rebecca had been at Aysgarth for just over a week and so far had made absolutely no progress at all in winning the twins' trust. They avoided her at every opportunity, and for the last two days the only time she had seen them had been at mealtimes and then later in the evening when, at her own insistence, she had helped Norty put them to bed.

Frazer had telephoned once during the week she had been there. On picking up the receiver and hearing his voice, she had been so paralysed with shock that she had been unable to do anything other than pass the receiver over to Mrs Norton. Luckily perhaps in the circumstances, because she had a pretty shrewd idea that neither the housekeeper nor Aunt Maud had seen fit to inform Frazer of the fact that his self-appointed governess to the children had left and that Rebecca had taken her place.

The sound of his voice had disturbed her more than she wanted to admit, at once so familiar and alien.

When Aunt Maud came to take the receiver from
the housekeeper to speak to her nephew, Rebecca
discovered that it was impossible for her to leave
the room. It was as though some invisible and painfully tight thread kept her within hearing distance
of his voice.

Dazedly she heard Aunt Maud confirm that she
and the twins were well, and although her brain
registered the fact that no mention was made either
of the governess's leaving or of her own arrival she
was feeling far too shocked to insist on Aunt
Maud's informing Frazer at once of her presence at
Aysgarth. That she herself was now party to the
deception that Maud was perpetrating against her
nephew only struck her when Maud finally replaced
the receiver.

'You didn't tell Frazer about my being here,' she
reminded the older woman wryly.

'Didn't I, dear?' Aunt Maud instantly fell back
on her prime means of defence, adopting a vague
and slightly puzzled attitude.

'No, you didn't,' Rebecca reaffirmed quietly.

For a moment Aunt Maud looked a little bit
guilty, then she said triumphantly, 'But, my dear,
he must know you were here. Mrs Norton told me
you'd answered the telephone.'

What could she say? How could she admit that
she had been so shocked emotionally by the sound

of his voice that her vocal cords had virtually become paralysed?

'I...I passed the receiver straight over to Mrs Norton,' she said uncomfortably, 'so I never actually spoke to Frazer.'

She bit her lip and then, much as it went against the grain to take to task this now elderly but still very awesome old lady for whom she still felt a slight residue of her childhood awe, she knew she had to tell her how uncomfortable she was about the fact that she was here at Aysgarth, living in Frazer's house without his knowledge, while being fully aware herself of how little he would want her there. And yet she wondered how to say as much in a way that would convince Aunt Maud that Frazer must be told and yet at the same time stop her asking any far too awkward questions about the nature of the supposed quarrel which had led to his reluctance to have her staying in the house.

To her relief and amazement, Aunt Maud took the burden of responsibility off her shoulders by patting her arm gently and saying in a kindly manner, 'You came here at my insistence, Rebecca, and to help me. If at a later stage Frazer should choose to take anyone to task about that, then, my dear, I'm afraid that my nephew is not the man I've always found him to be. In the absence of their parents and Frazer those children are my responsibility, and a responsibility which I take very seriously. But you can see for yourself that I'm far too old to keep an eye on them.'

Rebecca had to admit that this was true. Helen and Peter, while a little afraid of their great-aunt, were adept at manoeuvring themselves out of her presence. They had far, far more freedom than Rebecca remembered having at the same age, even here at Aysgarth.

Mrs Norton had told her on more than one occasion that they were regular little devils, especially, as she put it, 'Miss Helen'. Helen was the ringleader, the bolder of the two. Her awareness of the vulnerabilities and vanities that went up to make the adult psyche were far too great for a child of her own age, Rebecca considered.

'Perhaps a good boarding school might be the answer,' she suggested cautiously now, but Aunt Maud shook her head decisively.

'Don't think I haven't suggested it, my dear, but Frazer won't hear of it. He believes the children need the security of living at home.'

'But we all went to boarding school,' Rebecca protested.

'Yes, but Frazer contends that you all, especially you and Robert, had a far more secure and emotionally stable home background than the twins.'

Rebecca had to acknowledge that this was true;

but, while she could see Frazer's point in wanting to keep the twins at Aysgarth, she still wished she had not allowed herself to be dragooned into coming up here to share that responsibility.

'Don't worry, my dear,' Aunt Maud comforted her. 'I know you're finding things difficult at the moment, but I have every faith in your ability to bring those two to a proper realisation of at least a little discipline in their lives.'

Aunt Maud had more faith in her than she had in herself, Rebecca admitted ruefully. It had shaken her hearing Frazer's voice so unexpectedly like that, reminding her of things she had thought safely tucked away in the past. She had been fifteen when she first fell in love with him, dreamy-eyed and vague, her feelings more innocent and cerebral than physical.

She had likened him to all her favourite fictional heroes, had spent her holidays dreamily following him as much as she could, content to worship from afar. At sixteen her feelings had become sharper and far more painful; the physical awareness of her maturing body had both delighted and embarrassed her.

She remembered how the Christmas she was sixteen, when Frazer had bent to kiss her in the cousinly fashion that was his habit, she had ducked out of the way, petrified of betraying not just her feelings but her total lack of sophistication and experience. She so desperately wanted to be older, more experienced, more on what then had seemed to be Frazer's unattainably sophisticated level.

She remembered that that Christmas there had been a girl staying at Aysgarth—Frazer's latest girlfriend, a pretty and no doubt very pleasant girl, but Rebecca had invested her with all manner of unpleasant traits.

She had been desperately jealous of her and her relationship with Frazer. She remembered that she had refused to join the others on their annual walk to watch the Boxing Day meet set off. She remembered as well that, while Rory had jeered at her for being sulky and childish, Frazer had looked at her with thoughtful, concerned eyes. On reflection she realised that it was hardly surprising that he took his responsibility towards the twins so seriously. Even though only a handful of years had removed him in age from Rory, Robert and herself, he had always somehow or other seemed so very much more mature, a halfway stage between themselves and their parents.

She remembered her utter embarrassment when later that same holiday he had come up to her when she was sitting in her room daydreaming over an impossible sequence of events which concluded with him sweeping her into his arms and proclaiming his undying love. She remembered how he had knocked on her bedroom door and walked in, a tall dark-haired, jean-clad figure, wearing an old check woollen shirt, his body carrying the tang of fresh male sweat after his labours outside clearing a fresh fall of snow from the drive.

Rebecca remembered how her sensitive, newly emerging awareness had reacted to that very maleness of him; how a fierce thrill of pleasure had run through her as he sat down beside her on the window-seat. His first words to her, though, quickly dashed her foolish hopes.

He had come, he told her gently, to find out if something was wrong; if perhaps there was a problem at school. The knowledge that he so obviously still considered her to be a schoolgirl, a child, had been so bitterly painful that she had found it impossible to respond to anything he said, retreating further and further into her own protective shell, putting between them what she now recognised had been the beginning of a distance which neither of them had ever broached.

After that, with growing maturity, and aware of how potentially embarrassing for all concerned it would be if her feelings for him were ever to become public knowledge, she had made a point of avoiding him whenever she stayed at Aysgarth, spending more time in Rory's company than she did in Frazer's—and apparently so effectively convincing him that he was nothing more to her than merely an older and rather boring cousin that, when Rory had claimed she was the one with whom he was breaking his marriage vows, Frazer had had no difficulty whatsoever in believing him, which of course was exactly what she and Rory had wanted. So why afterwards had she felt that savage backlash of agonising pain that he should so easily have accepted their deceit? What had she expected him to do? Deny their claims and in doing so say passionately that he knew that she, Rebecca, could not possibly be involved with anyone else, because she loved him...and moreover that that love was returned?

How foolish she had been at eighteen! How naïve and unknown the reality of human emotions and reactions; male reactions in particular. Frazer's eruption of biting anger, followed by a tirade which had ultimately burned itself out and become an icy, unhidden contempt for both her and the relationship he believed she had had with his brother, had effectively destroyed for ever her still secretly cherished hope that one day he would turn to her and look at her with the eyes of love.

Driven beyond any reasonable caution by his reaction, she had told him fiercely that not for one moment did she regret her affair with Rory, and that she would love Rory for the rest of her life.

'You little fool!' he had told her with scathing contempt. 'Do you honestly believe that he feels the same way about you—a married man with one child already on the way?'

And then he had looked deliberately at her flat stomach and added, unforgivably, 'Or is it still only one?'

That night Rebecca had cried herself to sleep, wondering how it was that a man could be so blind that he couldn't instantly recognise her real feelings. That he couldn't instantly know that the only child she ever wanted to bear was his.

That morning he had come up to her room as he had done once before, but this time not to ask her gently what it was that troubled her, but to tell her coldly and emotionlessly that he felt it best that she pack her bags and immediately leave Aysgarth.

She had done so, numbed, frozen to the heart by this total rejection of her, and as the taxi he had ordered for her drove her away from Aysgarth she had not turned round once to look behind her, knowing that if she did her view would only be distorted by the tears already blurring her vision. Since then she had not been back.

Oh, they had met at the twins' christening and at Robert's wedding, but on neither of these occasions had they done more than exchange coolly hostile smiles of acknowledgement, and then only with the safe distance of the width of a room and several intermediate relatives between them.

Robert had tried awkwardly to bring them back together, sensing perhaps more than anyone else what Frazer's rejection of her was doing to her. No one, apart from Rory, knew the real truth about the reason for their mutual hostility.

Just as he had announced that she was no longer welcome at Aysgarth, and his word was absolute law, so he had also stated that in no circumstances whatsoever was the fact that she and Rory had been indulging in an illicit and contemptible affair to become public knowledge. It was enough, he had told her, that he knew, and he had already undertaken to make sure that Rory's wife was kept in the dark about her husband's perfidious behaviour.

Another stern lecture had followed, this time on the vulnerability of women carrying their first child, and Rebecca had wept inwardly while standing straight and apparently uncaring beneath the biting lash of his words.

As far as the rest of the family were concerned, a mutual disagreement had led to their estrangement; a quarrel which neither of them cared to talk about but which both of them made it clear to other

members of the family had been important enough
to keep them apart.

Sometimes Rebecca suspected that Robert
guessed that there was far more to it than that. They
had been close as children, probably closer than
most brothers and sisters, because of the fact that
their parents were living abroad. Robert was five
years her senior, just a year older than Rory, and
Rebecca suspected that he had a good idea exactly
how she really felt about Frazer. If so, he had the
tact at least not to say so, but on the occasion of
his marriage to Ailsa she had been bitterly conscious of the fact that Robert was doing his best to
push her and Frazer together.

He had asked Frazer to act as his best man and
she, Rebecca, had been Ailsa's chief bridesmaid. It
had been only natural that the two of them should
be paired together during the wedding, festivities.
There had been one moment when, hand under her
elbow, to guide her towards their places at the top
table, Frazer had bent his head just sufficiently to
say threateningly against her ear, 'Remember, this
is supposed to be a happy occasion, Rebecca. For
Robert and Ailsa's sake at least, try to look as
though you're enjoying yourself. You and I both
know quite well that you would much prefer Rory
to be here at your side, but that,' he had told her
silkily, and with obvious pleasure, 'is impossible.

Unfortunately for you, you chose to love the wrong man.'

Rebecca had thought bitterly then how right he was, and, watching the happiness emanating from her brother and new sister-in-law, she had made herself a vow there and then that from now on she would cut herself free of the past, and more especially from her idiotic and totally foolish feelings for Frazer.

Until now she had thought she had succeeded, if not totally, then at least with a very creditable measure of success. All it had taken to show her just how much she had been deceiving herself was the mere sound of Frazer's voice.

If the sound of his voice could affect her so compellingly, what would happen if she was ever forced to confront him, to come face to face with the physical presence of him? Assuring herself that this was hardly likely to happen, she told herself that she would be far better employed directing her mental energy towards finding a way of dealing with the twins.

So far, despite all her overtures, she was no closer to establishing any kind of rapport with them; but now it wasn't merely her professional pride that was being affected by their resistance to her; she was also seriously concerned for the twins themselves, and more especially for Helen, because she was beginning to see how emotionally and dangerously isolated the two of them were becoming.

Such intense emotional dependence on one another was not a good thing. Both of them needed to form friendships with other children of their own age, but as far as she could see there was no chance of that being achieved, although she had suggested on numerous occasions during the time that she had been at Aysgarth that she was quite happy to take one or both of them to visit their school friends. Her offer had not been taken up, and it had been Peter who had innocently and unawarely confirmed her own impression of the truth by saying one morning that neither he nor Helen had any friends.

'We don't need any,' Helen added, fiercely clutching at her brother's arm. 'We've got each other.'

Further conversation with Aunt Maud had elicited the fact that their headmaster at their local school had also indicated concern about the twins' intense emotional bonding to one another.

'Frazer's tried to encourage them to make other friends,' Maud told her, 'but we're so isolated here.'

It frustrated Rebecca to know that three months was nowhere near long enough for her to win the twins' confidence and to help them establish the kind of emotional independence from one another

which they would need to enable them to lead
healthily emotional adult lives.

Without warning or meaning to, she found herself becoming more and more emotionally involved
with them, wanting to help them, knowing how to
help them but totally unable to penetrate the defensive measures both of them, but more especially
Helen, threw up against her. She knew quite well
that they spent a lot of time in the woods and down
by the river, but was reluctant to penetrate their
privacy, fearing that it would do more harm than
good to force her company upon them. So instead
she tried casually mentioning all sorts of hobbies
and activities, hoping that she might hit on one
which would tempt the twins enough to accept her
company.

One morning she thought that she might have
succeeded when she mentioned casually at the
breakfast table that she rather fancied going riding.

'Do they still have that riding stables down at
Ottershot?' she asked Aunt Maud as she helped herself to coffee and buttered a piece of toast.

'I think so,' her aunt confirmed. 'Mrs Scott, the
vicar's wife, would probably know. She seems to
keep her finger on the pulse of everything that's
going on locally. Why don't you give her a ring?'

'I think I might,' Rebecca confirmed. 'It's ages

since I've been riding. Those are the kind of things I miss most in London.'

All the time she was speaking, she was aware of Helen's interested and yet resentful attention focusing on her. Apparently casually, she turned to the twins and enquired, 'Do either of you ride?'

'Helen does,' Peter piped up, and was, she suspected, abruptly kicked on the ankle by his twin for his pains.

'No, I don't,' Helen denied abruptly and rudely. 'I hate riding!'

She pushed away her plate and flung herself off her chair, and watching her stiff-backed departure from the room, Rebecca reflected wryly that the little girl might just as well have said 'I hate you,' because that had been what she meant.

'Oh dear,' Aunt Maud said tiredly, watching Peter follow his sister. 'They're such a very difficult pair of children. I don't know whether it's me who's getting older, Rebecca, but I don't remember any of you being quite as difficult to deal with as these two.'

Rebecca touched her aunt's arm comfortingly.

'I expect we were all every bit as naughty,' she told her, 'but we were lucky, especially Robert and me. Both of us were happy enough at school, and then we had the reassurance of knowing our parents loved and missed us.'

'Yes, I'm afraid Rory and Lillian are very remiss in that area,' Aunt Maud confessed. 'I suppose it's old-fashioned of me, but I really can't understand these modern marriages. Both Rory and Lillian say quite openly, and in front of the children, that they don't get on, and yet Lillian is out in Hong Kong with Rory, whereas I would have thought in such circumstances she would have preferred to stay here in this country with the children.'

It had always been Rebecca's private view that Lillian loved Rory very much indeed, and she suspected that it was her fear of losing her errant husband that kept her at his side and not in England with the twins.

'Children are like animals,' Aunt Maud continued. 'They always seem to know when they aren't loved.'

When Rebecca protested that she was sure that both Rory and Lillian did love their children, Aunt Maud sighed and admitted, 'Yes, possibly they do in their own way, but, although I don't like saying so even to you, it's a very selfish way, Rebecca, and selfish not just to the children but to Frazer as well. He's virtually become the twins' father, and yet because he's the man he is he's scrupulous about not trying to take what he perceives as Rory's rightful place in their lives. He's the only person that the twins really seem to respond to, and Helen in particular.'

'But one day he's going to marry and have children of his own, which will make Helen feel doubly rejected,' Rebecca inserted, sighing.

Aunt Maud looked at her and said quietly, 'Yes, I'm afraid so. That's why I think it's essential that both of them learn to admit other people into their lives. That's why I asked you to come up here, Rebecca,' she added. 'You aren't just another stranger who's been hired by their parents to take charge of them. You're a member of their family as well.'

'A member of their family whom they don't want to accept,' Rebecca told her ruefully.

Aunt Maud sighed and patted her hand.

'Give it time, child,' she counselled. 'Give it time.'

Amazingly, the very evening after that conversation something happened that seemed to indicate that at last Rebecca had made a breakthrough. She had been talking with Aunt Maud about her own childhood memories of Aysgarth, hoping through her conversation with her great-aunt to establish some point of contact with the twins, who were silently watching television.

'I used to love the valley in particular, and the

river,' she commented, her attention supposedly on her great-aunt but in fact on the twins.

'I know you did,' Aunt Maud agreed grimly. 'I seem to remember there was more than one occasion on which you came back soaking wet!'

Rebecca laughed, genuinely amused by her own sudden recollections of the incidents Aunt Maud was referring to.

'Yes,' she agreed, 'I remember once when Rory and Robert punished me for interrupting one of their games by throwing me into the shallow part of the river. Luckily Frazer saw them and rescued me.'

'We like the valley and the river too, don't we, Peter?'

Startled, Rebecca turned to look at her. The little girl had turned round and was facing her. The novelty of actually being addressed by the child without having to draw a response from her silenced Rebecca for a moment, then she said cautiously, 'Do you?'

Peter too had now turned round, and he said enthusiastically, 'Yes, we do. Frazer's taught us both to fish, but we aren't allowed to go fishing without him.'

Anxious to grasp the moment before it slipped away, Rebecca said quickly, 'Well, perhaps I could take you fishing.'

She couldn't help noticing the way Peter looked quickly at his sister for her response before making any of his own. To her surprise and delight, after pausing for a moment, Helen said slowly, 'Yes, all right.'

'We'll go tomorrow afternoon,' Rebecca promised them. 'Perhaps we could make some sandwiches and have a picnic down there.'

Later on in the evening, still light-headed with the relief of having finally made contact with them, she confessed to Aunt Maud, 'At last! I really was beginning to think they would never accept me.'

Conscious of the fact that neither Mrs Norton nor Aunt Maud were getting any younger and two young children and an adult represented quite an additional burden on the household, Rebecca had insisted on taking over doing the shopping, which was why she had suggested to the twins that they leave their fishing expedition until the afternoon.

Having arranged that she would have a quick snack lunch in the local market town, while carrying out all Mrs Norton's and Aunt Maud's commissions, she arrived home with just under half an hour in which to unpack and put away the shopping and get ready to meet the twins. She made it with only a couple of minutes to spare, hurriedly pulling on a pair of old worn jeans and a thin T-shirt, but when she went downstairs she discovered from Mrs Norton that the twins had already left.

'I told them they should wait for you,' she told Rebecca, 'but so headstrong they are, the pair of them, especially Miss Helen. She said to tell you they'd meet you down by the weir.'

'The weir!' Rebecca frowned.

'They've taken the little rods Mr Frazer got for them,' Mrs Norton added, and Rebecca, who suspected that she would spend far more of the afternoon helping the children to catch their fish than catching any of her own, nodded her head and said quickly, 'I'd better get down there. How long have they been gone?'

'No more than ten minutes at the most,' Mrs Norton assured her.

Telling herself that she was being idiotic to worry, when it was obvious that both children virtually roamed the estate at will, nevertheless Rebecca found as she descended the steep slope that led immediately into the valley that her heart was pounding with nervous tension and anxiety for the twins' safety.

Approximately halfway down the hill, there was a small gap in the trees and scree through which it was possible to have an uninterrupted view of the weir pool. Out of force of habit, Rebecca paused there.

The pool, always deceptively calm and unruffled on the surface, masking the true danger of the very strong current below, shimmered in the afternoon sunlight. And then, as she watched, she saw something floating on its surface. Her heart somersaulted quickly, her pulses starting to pound with shock as she recognised Peter's distinctive red and blue lightweight jacket floating on the surface of the pond.

She started to run, automatically dodging shrubs and trees, unaware of scratches and blows to her skin, her one thought to reach that small and all too vulnerable figure floating on the surface of the pond before it was too late. Old habits died hard, and Frazer had lectured them all to good purpose.

At the pool's edge, she stopped to kick off her shoes and remove her jacket. Her jeans and top would take too long to remove and should not get in the way when she was swimming.

She dived in and swam strongly towards the familiar red blob. After Frazer had warned them about the dangers of swimming in the weir pond, she had always felt an inner terror of the apparently calm water, which seemed all the more threatening because of the placid face it presented to the world while such danger lurked below.

The currents were caused in the main by the sluices which opened to allow the overspill of water to float out through the weir, and after the heavy spring and early summer rainfall the currents were flowing very fast indeed. Rebecca herself could feel the strong pull of them as she swam swiftly towards Peter, praying as she did so that she was not too late to prevent him being sucked into the current and swept over the weir and that he was still alive.

How on earth he came to be in the water in the first place, she had no idea. She knew that the twins had been warned about the dangers of the weir. All she could think was that they had attempted to start fishing without her and that somehow or other Peter had fallen in.

She was close to the edge of the weir now. She could hear the noise the water made as it poured over the edge and dropped well over forty feet into the river below—or was the noise she could hear the terrified pounding of her own heart?

Peter, lighter in weight than her, an inert small body, unable to do anything to help himself, was already caught up in the fast flow of the current, and it was only with a gigantic physical effort that Rebecca was actually able to increase her speed and reach out despairingly to grab hold of the jacket.

In the cold shock of finding it empty, she forgot about the current and her own potential danger and knew only a sharp fearing dread for Peter and his safety. As she clung to the jacket, something hard and painfully sharp rasped her bare arm, shocking her into awareness of her own danger.

The current had caught her and driven her hard up against the barrier of the weir. At the same moment as she realised what was happening, a voice hailed her from the shore, causing her to flounder as she turned her head and stared disbelievingly at the furious dark-haired man standing there. Frazer! Frazer here!

But he couldn't be. That was impossible—he was in America. As she fought frantically against the current, more frightened now of Frazer's anger at finding her at Aysgarth than the danger of the strong current, she saw that he had pulled off his jacket and was removing his shoes. She made a last desperate effort to free herself from the current and succeeded in propelling her body out of immediate danger and into slightly calmer water.

It wasn't enough, though, to prevent Frazer from diving cleanly into the water, and combined with her sick feeling of shock as he caught up with her and firmly took hold of her was an unwanted feeling of weak relief. As he towed her back to the shore, she tried to tell him about Peter, but in doing so swallowed so much water that by the time he had got her ashore, she was too weak to do anything other than retch uncomfortably.

He pushed her unceremoniously on to the ground

as she struggled to sit up and tell him about Peter, and then to discover herself the object of a brisk and thoroughly professional demonstration of first aid rendered it impossible for her to do anything other than lie there shivering and sick.

Frazer too was silent, although as she tried to focus on him and his features swam in and out of her dazed consciousness, Rebecca was bitterly aware of the grim look of anger in his eyes.

As she lay there soaked and shivering, she became aware of something else as well. There were two matching pairs of sandals just within her line of vision; two matching pairs of bare brown legs and also two matching pairs of dark green shorts. As she raised her head, she saw the twins standing together looking down at her, and above and beyond her relief that they were safe was the overwhelming realisation that Peter's jacket had deliberately been thrown into the weir, and she, like the fool that she was, had reacted just as they wanted. What an idiot she had been to believe that Helen had given way so easily!

As she had done before, she acquitted the little girl of realising the true extent of the danger she had been in. No doubt Helen had thought that a thorough soaking and the blow to her pride would probably be enough to send her high-tailing it back to London. She lay back on the ground and closed her eyes. Too much had happened too quickly for her to be able to take it all in.

A feeling of numbness crept through her body, accompanied by an equally unpleasant feeling of nausea. Her ears buzzed, and although she tried desperately to hold on to it she felt her consciousness slipping away. In the distance she heard Peter asking anxiously, 'She isn't going to die, is she?'

CHAPTER FOUR

WHEN she came round, Rebecca was still lying on the ground. Her body felt icy cold although her head was a little clearer. Something was coming between her and the warmth of the sun. No, not something but someone, she recognised as she opened her eyes and saw Frazer standing grimly over her.

'What the devil possessed you to go into the pool like that?' he demanded savagely. 'You know how dangerous it is!'

'Peter...' she croaked, but he overruled her attempt to explain, saying ruthlessly,

'Peter had lost his jacket—so what? If I hadn't happened to be on my way down here, you'd quite probably have drowned,' he told her brutally, and added sarcastically, 'or were you expecting the twins to jump in and save you?'

Wincing under the bitter lash of his voice, Rebecca struggled to sit up. It was bad enough that he was here at all and had witnessed her stupidity, without her adding to her own indignity and vulnerability by lying on the ground at his feet. She winced as she sat up, the abrasions on her tender skin painful. Out of the corner of her eye, she saw the anxious, guilty expressions on Helen and Peter's faces. Peter looked almost sick with shock and fear. Helen was more stalwart, but there was no mistaking the little girl's realisation of how very badly her trick could have turned out.

Wearily acknowledging that there was little point in telling the truth—at best he would probably only condemn her for being stupid enough to be taken in by it at the first place, and she felt that the twins had learned a very valuable lesson—without looking at them she said as casually as she could, 'Yes, it was stupid of me.'

Frazer was obviously not placated.

'It was more than stupid,' he told her coldly. 'You do realise, don't you, that you could have risked the twins' lives as well as your own? What if one of them had tried to follow you in there?'

There was more irony in her voice than she knew when she said drily, 'Oh, I don't think they'd have done that.'

'No,' Frazer agreed icily, 'they're far too sensible to do anything so criminally foolish.'

He saw that she was shivering violently and frowned, directing the twins, 'Run up to the house

and ask Mrs Norton to prepare a hot water bottle
and a bath for Rebecca, will you?'

Cravenly, Rebecca didn't want to be left alone
with him. The physical danger she had been in
might have got her over the initial shock of seeing
him so unexpectedly, but she had very little doubt
that sooner or later she was going to be called to
account for her presence at Aysgarth.

As she struggled to get up, Frazer commanded
her curtly, 'Stay there, I'll carry you up to the
house.'

Carry her? As she looked up at him disbelievingly, he smiled back at her grimly and bent to pick
her up, not in any tender facsimile of a lover's embrace, but instead in a very undignified and also
uncomfortable fireman's lift. So much for the fierce
thud of panic her heart had given at the thought of
being held in his arms, Rebecca reflected grimly as
she was carried relentlessly up the hill towards the
house.

The twins, Mrs Norton and Aunt Maud were all
waiting there for them in varying states of anxiety.
Aunt Maud's normally high colour had gone, leaving her face pale, and as Frazer dismissed both
women's anxious queries as to her state of health,
refusing their offers of help, he said coldly to her
once they were out of sight of the waiting quartet,
'Yes, now you think of Aunt Maud's age. A pity

you didn't think of that before. She's not a young woman any more.'

He pushed open the door of her bedroom and dumped her down on the bed as though she were nothing more than a sack of coal, she reflected angrily, stung into retaliating swiftly, 'No, she isn't, which is something you might have thought of before you dumped the twins on her and went swanning off to the States!'

As he frowned down at her, she cursed her unruly tongue, wondering what on earth had prompted her to retaliate so recklessly. His response was surprisingly mild.

'I didn't dump them on her, as you put it,' he told her quite calmly. 'In fact I left an extremely competent and, so I thought, responsible young woman here in charge of them.'

'She left,' Rebecca told him coldly.

There was a moment's silence; then he said, 'Yes, I know. That's the reason I'm here. She got in touch with me to let me know what had happened. Although she felt she couldn't possibly continue to look after the twins, she felt it her duty to let me know the reasons why she'd felt obliged to leave. Naturally, the moment I realised that Aunt Maud was on her own here looking after them, I cancelled the rest of the tour and made arrangements to come home, only to find...'

'Only to find that your sacrifice was completely unnecessary,' Rebecca suggested sweetly, 'since Aunt Maud had already made alternative arrangements.'

The look he gave her was derisive and hurtful.

'If this afternoon's episode was anything to go by, I hardly think that your tender care of the twins is of a type to banish parental fears.'

There were so many things she could have said, but what would be the point? Frazer was determined to see the very worst of her. The pain of knowing that made the blood leave her face. She shivered, chilled to the bone, shaking with reaction now that the immediacy of her ordeal was over.

'What you need is a hot bath,' Frazer told her crisply, monitoring her reaction. 'Can you manage on your own, or....'

For a moment Rebecca actually thought that he was suggesting he should help her, and her face flamed scarlet at the thought of his hands on her body, no matter how impersonally. As though he could read her mind he said quietly, 'If you do need help, I can always ask Mrs Norton.'

She shook her head, sending drops of water spraying on to the bedding. One droplet landed on Frazer's hand, and as she watched he glanced at it, then casually lifted his hand to his mouth, licking the moisture away, a simple, almost absentminded gesture but one which made her stomach churn in mute reaction to the wantonness of her own thoughts.

Frazer got up and walked towards the door, pausing there to turn round and say acidly, 'Why did you come here, Rebecca?'

She purposely chose to misunderstand him, shrugging her shoulders and saying coolly, 'Because Aunt Maud asked me to.'

The look he gave her warned her that it was not the answer he was prepared to accept, but before he could question her any further Mrs Norton came bustling in, carrying a mug of steaming tea.

'Drink this up, dear,' she said to Rebecca. 'It's got plenty of sugar in for shock.'

Obediently Rebecca took the mug from her, allowing the housekeeper to fuss over her as Frazer opened the door and let himself out of her room. Despite her objections, he insisted on summoning the doctor.

It seemed to Rebecca, her nerves stretched to their limits, first with the shock of believing that Peter was drowning and then by the arrival of Frazer, that the doctor took an unconscionably long time in his examination, sounding her chest and then frowning thoughtfully before removing his stethoscope.

'Tell me,' he invited, when he had finished, 'have

you suffered from any kind of lung or breathing infection in the last twelve months? Bronchitis, pneumonia…anything like that?'

Uncomfortably Rebecca admitted, 'I had pneumonia last winter.'

She still felt guilty about the way she had ignored the symptoms, which had eventually become so bad that she had earned herself not only a severe lecture from her own doctor, but a rather prolonged stay in bed. Her excuse had been that she had been so busy that she had simply not dared take time off.

'Mm…' Was the doctor's only comment, but the look he gave her spoke volumes, and Rebecca felt her heart sink as he turned his head and said firmly to Frazer, 'I'm afraid your cousin is going to have to stay in bed—at least for the next few days.' He then turned back to her and told Rebecca herself, 'And the reason that I'm telling *Frazer* that you're to stay in bed is that I suspect that, if I don't, you'll be up and dressed the moment I turn my back.'

'There's nothing seriously wrong, is there?' Frazer interrupted him.

He might at least have had the good manners to leave her alone with the doctor, Rebecca reflected bitterly, watching him. He was making her feel rather like a recalcitrant child, not the adult she was…both of them talking about her as though she wasn't there.

'Not at this stage,' the doctor assured him, 'but there's just a suggestion of difficulty there I shouldn't want to see developing. Pneumonia is an extremely debilitating disease, even for a woman as young and otherwise healthy as your cousin. A little cautiousness now will cost nothing.' He got up and gave Rebecca a reassuring smile; an ageing, tired-looking man who she could tell took his responsibilities to his patients very much to heart.

She knew she ought to be grateful to him for reminding her of the fact that she had been very seriously ill indeed earlier in the year...something which she herself tended to push to the back of her mind; as much because it made her realise how very silly she had been as because of her unpleasant memories of the uncomfortable time she had spent fighting off the infection.

She had only narrowly escaped being admitted to hospital, and then only because her mother had insisted on taking her home and nursing her herself.

She had not given that illness a thought when she had seen Peter's jacket floating on the surface of the pool, but now suddenly, as thought the doctor's warning words had conjured it up out of nowhere, she found that she was shivering fitfully, and that her chest felt uncomfortably tight.

'I'll leave a prescription,' the doctor was saying to Frazer, then he turned to Rebecca and said quietly, 'The tightness *should* ease within a couple of days. I'll call in tomorrow to check how you're doing.'

He got up and turned to leave before she could object and tell him that she was all right. And she was all right…or at least she had been until he started prodding and poking at her, she thought in blurry resentment.

Her head was starting to ache; a dull, heavy ache, accompanied by the feeling that it was stuffed with a thick material that made it impossible for her to think properly. She wanted to cough, but when she did so, her chest hurt.

She was still coughing when Frazer walked back into her room, although now the spasm was easing, leaving in its wake a depressingly familiar shakiness combined with a foolish urge to burst into tears.

Frazer took one look at her and said scathingly, 'All this for a child's jacket! Was it really worth it?'

Not for a child's jacket, no, but for a child's life, yes. The words burned the tip of her tongue, but heroically she swallowed them. Although she would have given a great deal to wipe the cynical look from Frazer's eyes, she could not do so by exposing the twins. She was quite convinced that neither of them realised the seriousness of their actions. She had seen their frightened, chastened expressions when Frazer brought her out of the water.

She took a deep breath without thinking, trying to steady rioting emotions, and gasped out loud as pain clutched her lungs and compressed her chest.

Instinctively she fought for breath, Frazer virtually forgotten as she raised herself up on her pillows, fighting against the iron pressure gripping her body, her panic now far greater than it had been when she was in the water and had had a goal to aim for.

And then miraculously someone was helping her, telling her calmly to breathe slowly, easing her body into a position that relaxed the vicious grip on her chest, allowing the life-saving air to fill her lungs.

It was several seconds before she was stable enough to recognise that the soothing hands and voice belonged to Frazer. He was still standing beside her bed, his face unexpectedly tense as he watched her.

'Does that happen often?' he demanded tersely.

Rebecca managed a weak smile.

'Only when I go in swimming in unheated pools,'

She saw that he wasn't amused, and that if anything he looked even more tense.

'You had asthma as a child,' he said, frowning at her, the words almost an accusation.

'Very mildly,' she agreed calmly. 'And only for a very short time.'

But he didn't appear to be listening to her. He was pacing the floor, and he turned to fling at her,

'Asthma, pneumonia…and you still go virtually drowning yourself in water which you know damn well comes straight down off the mountains and is ice-cold! What are you, Rebecca?'

'Forgetful,' she hazarded, but her attempt at humour met with no response other than a fiercely frowning look.

'You realise that if I hadn't been there you could easily have…'

'…drowned,' she supplied drily for him, suddenly too exhausted to keep up a pretence any longer. 'Don't try to pretend you'd have mourned me if I had,' she said bitterly. 'What was it you said to me when you told me what you thought of my relationship with Rory? That hanging was too good for me.'

To her surprise she saw that her words must have caught Frazer on a raw spot, because a dull surge of colour burned briefly along his cheekbones.

At eighteen she had thought him invulnerable, invincible, had looked on him more as a god than a man. Now she realised her perceptions were sharper, more mature...now she could see him without the deceptive veils of adoration and youth.

So much had changed in the years they had been estranged. *She* had changed, and so perhaps had he...but one thing had not changed, she acknowledged unhappily. One thing remained fixed and indestructible. Her blind adoration of him might have gone, but the feeling that had been at its core, the pain she had called love—that was still there.

She shivered, looking not at him, but past him, her grey eyes suddenly sad and pensive, unaware of how vulnerable and fragile she looked. Her normally sleek shoulder-length blonde hair curled softly round her make-up-less face. Her skin, always pale, now looked virtually bloodless; only her mouth was full and soft, betraying a rich colour starkly at oddness with her paleness.

'I was furious, both with you and with Rory.' She heard the words and focused on Frazer's face 'For God's sake, Rebecca, no matter what you felt for him, you knew he was a married man!'

She could hear the anger in his voice, feel the vibrations of it almost just as she had done so long ago. Exhausted, and suddenly desperately anxious to be alone, she turned her head away and said threadily, 'I don't want to talk about it.'

'No, you never did want to face up to reality, did you?' Frazer accused. 'You always were a daydreamer, living more in your imagination than in reality. What did you tell yourself, Rebecca? That Lillian simply didn't exist? Or didn't you even care that much?'

'Why accuse me?' she suddenly fired up, using her last precious reserves of energy. 'I wasn't some seductress, deliberately enchanting Rory away from Lillian. It does take two...'

'Yes,' he agreed heavily. 'But I thought that, even at eighteen, you had the intelligence and the perception to be aware of Rory's weaknesses.'

'If it hadn't been me, it would have been someone else,' she told him quietly, wondering if he would hear beneath her words her plea to him to let the past die.

If he *had* he was ignoring it, because he replied harshly, 'Maybe, but it *was* you. Can't you understand...?'

He broke off as the door opened and Aunt Maud came in.

'Forgive me for interrupting, Frazer dear, but I was anxious to hear what the doctor had to say.'

'He says I'm fine,' Rebecca assured her before Frazer could speak. 'And now that Frazer's back, I might as well leave.'

'Not yet,' Frazer contradicted her flatly. 'Not until the doctor has agreed that you're well enough to do so.'

'Oh, dear!' Aunt Maud looked unhappy. 'I feel this is all my fault. If I hadn't asked for your help...'

'It isn't your fault at all, Maud,' Frazer reassured the older woman before Rebecca could speak. 'Rebecca is perfectly well aware of the dangers of the weir pool.'

He put his arm around his aunt's shoulders, at once both protecting her and guiding her towards the door, and Rebecca felt her eyes stinging with ridiculous tears for her own envy and vulnerability.

As they reached the door, Aunt Maud had rallied enough to say firmly, 'There was no need for you to come home, you know, dear. Rebecca and I were managing perfectly well. That girl had no right to get in touch with you.'

'On the contrary, she showed exemplary responsibility and forethought,' Frazer continued crisply. 'Which was exactly why I employed her in the first place. Why exactly did you dismiss her?'

Maud dismiss her! Rebecca pricked up her ears. According to the story she had been told, the girl had resigned; left of her own free will almost overnight.

Aunt Maud was making some vague and totally confusing response and, as he opened the door, she heard Frazer asking briskly, 'Well, never mind, we'll discuss it later. By the way, can you remember what we did with that camp bed we used to have?'

Rebecca had no idea what on earth Frazer could want with a camp bed, and she was too tired to really care. Her emotions had been seesawing up and down ever since his arrival. She felt so drained emotionally that she was almost thankful that he had gone, even though in leaving he had robbed her of the secret agony of allowing her senses to drink in the physical reality of him. Odd that, while she had remembered some things so clearly, like his anger and his contempt, she had forgotten others, like the way his mouth curled when it was softened with compassion...like the way he moved, lithely and very malely; like the way he smelled, clean and yet at the same time subtly erotic.

He must have been very concerned indeed to have broken his tour, she mused as she lay there. No doubt once he had evicted her from Aysgarth, he would find another governess to take charge of the twins and return to America.

She had a very strong suspicion that were it not for the doctor she would have already found herself on her way home.

Pride urged her to make as fast a recovery as she could so that she could leave of her own free will. She looked longingly at the wardrobe that held her clothes and suitcase, wondering if she had the strength to get up and pack. She need not go very far. There were enough places within half an hour or so's drive that let rooms on a bed and breakfast basis, surely, for her to get a bed for the night.

Once the thought was born it wouldn't go away. The pleasure of outmanoeuvring Frazer, of leaving before he could demand the removal of her presence, was too tempting for her to resist.

She got out of bed, pleased to discover that she was more steady on her feet than she had expected, even though it did take her rather a long time to cross the ridiculously small space to the wardrobe, and she had to stop once to ease the pain in her chest.

Once there she did feel oddly weak, but she refused to allow that to deter her. She opened the wardrobe and removed her suitcase, then laboriously started packing.

She had removed less than half a dozen items when her chest suddenly became ominously tight. She tried to stand up and found she couldn't. Mentally telling herself not to panic, she tried to breathe slowly and deeply, trying not to think of the fact that she was completely alone and that through her own folly had put herself in a very dangerous position indeed.

The pain gripping her lungs refused to ease. She could only draw in cautious sips of air. When her bedroom door opened slowly and cautiously, she forgot about controlling her breathing, and consequently, when the twins came in, they found her fighting for breath, and the sight and sound of her struggles was enough to send them running to find Frazer.

Idiotically, by the time he came, the attack was over, and she had all but managed to make it back to bed.

'What the hell do you think you're doing?' were the words with which he greeted her as he burst into the room, the twins behind him. 'Do you *want* to kill yourself?'

He saw the open wardrobe and the clothes spilling from it and his mouth tightened ominously.

'You're a fool, do you know that?' he demanded as he walked across the floor and unceremoniously picked her up.

Now, with her eyes on a level with his and his heart beating oddly unsteadily beneath the hand she had placed on his chest to push herself away from him, Rebecca found it impossible to speak. She was far too aware of all the subtle messages her body was giving her; and some of them not so subtle, she recognised in cringing mortification as she felt the unmistakable surge of arousal flood her body.

'What do you think it would do to Aunt Maud

if she found out you'd half killed yourself trying to leave? Have you no consideration?'

Had *she* no consideration!

She gritted her teeth against all the bitter accusatory words she wanted to fling at him as she remembered that they had an interested audience. Well, at least the twins must be in no doubt now about the true nature of her relationship with Frazer.

As though he picked up on her thoughts, Frazer turned to them and said firmly, 'OK, you two, it's well past your bedtime. Baths, please...at once... and then I'll be up to read your story.'

They obeyed him immediately, Rebecca noticed wryly.

As he placed her back on her bed with more urgency than finesse he said brusquely, 'No more heroics, if you don't mind. I might be able to see through them, but Maud can't.'

If she had ever once hoped that a miracle might occur, that he might somehow see through his own prejudices and perceive the truth, or, even more unlikely, that he would mentally lay waste to the barriers he had erected between them and, metaphorically at least, welcome her back with open arms into the circle of those he trusted and loved, Rebecca realised now the extent of her self-indulgent folly.

Frazer would never allow her to forget the past—

for one very good reason. He himself did not want to forget it. It was almost as though in some way he actually took a certain bitter pleasure in remembering it.

She told herself that the tears stinging her eyes came more from exhaustion and physical weakness than from emotional pain, turning her head away from him so that he wouldn't see them as she muttered defiantly, 'You wanted me to leave.'

What was it about him that drove her into reacting like a recalcitrant child? Far better to have simply ignored his comment and let him go. Far better, far more mature, far safer. Because now he had turned and was looking back at the bed, his eyes narrowing speculatively as though he too was wondering why she was prolonging their intimacy.

'Yes,' he agreed unequivocally. 'But only when you're physically well enough to do so. You can turn yourself into a martyr if you want to, Rebecca, but don't expect me to help you do it.'

'You still hate me, don't you?' she burst out unwisely, overwrought and dangerously close to the edge of losing her self-control.

'Hate you? He smiled at her, a cold, taunting smile that made her feel sick inside. 'No, I don't hate you at all, Rebecca. Hatred, after all, is a very powerful emotion. If I feel anything for you, I suppose it's a mixture of pity and contempt. Pity because you were silly enough to fall for Rory and contempt because you allowed yourself to become involved with him even though you knew he was married.'

'*Allowed* myself? People don't *allow* themselves to fall in love, Frazer!'

'Yes, they do,' he countered coolly. 'There's always a point early on in such a relationship where one has the option to draw back or go on. That point should have come for you the moment you realised what Rory was doing. You knew he wasn't free.'

'*I* should have drawn back! *I* knew! So it was all my fault, was it?' she demanded recklessly.

For a moment something dark and painful touched his face and a feeling unlike anything she had ever known before hit the pit of her stomach, a mingling of yearning, rage, and helpless, hopeless love.

'No,' he said slowly, 'it wasn't all your fault. I blame myself just as much. I should have seen what was happening, but I...'

'You were too involved in your own love life,' she supplied for him.

The look he gave her shocked her, it was so bitter and acid.

'Yes,' he agreed grittily. 'So involved that I was virtually blind to what was going on under my nose.

You've never married, nor been seriously involved with anyone else, if family gossip is to be believed,' he added curtly. 'If that means that you're still carrying a torch for Rory...'

'That's my affair, and I'm not prepared to discuss it with you!' Rebecca interrupted him sharply. She had endured enough, and even if it was her own fault for instituting the argument in the first place, she felt she had been punished sufficiently. To hear Frazer telling her of his pity and contempt for her...

She knew that if he didn't leave her soon she was likely to disgrace herself by bursting into tears in front of him.

'I'm tired, Frazer,' she told him unnecessarily, unaware of the haunting fragility of her face and the shadows that lay like bruises against her skin, making the man watching her suddenly aware of how very slender she had become and how very vulnerable she looked.

He walked to the door in silence and opened it, pausing only when Rebecca said shakily, 'And you needn't worry—the moment the doctor tells me I'm well enough to leave, I'll be ready to go.'

It was only after he had gone that she acknowledged the shock it must have given him to come home and find her here. No wonder he had been so furious with her when he fished her out of the pool! She wondered if he had been tempted to simply let her drown, and then she acknowledged that such behaviour was not and could never be a part of his character. Frazer believed in confronting the problems in his life, not sidestepping them or, even worse, ignoring them as Rory was inclined to do.

The two brothers could not really have been more different. Rory so lightweight and beneath his surface charm so deeply selfish; Frazer on the surface the harsher and far less appealing of the two, but in reality, at least where others who were not herself were concerned, so deeply compassionate and aware.

She wondered if he still loved Michelle. He must do, since he had never made any attempt to build a commitment with anyone else. When, months after the débâcle of her confrontation with Frazer, she had finally managed to pluck up the courage to say vaguely to her mother that she supposed Frazer and Michelle must soon be setting a date for the wedding, her mother had looked astonished and announced that the relationship was over and that Michelle had apparently gone to work in New York.

Rebecca had not been entirely surprised. After all, if Michelle had secretly been having an affair with Rory she had obviously not been wholly committed to Frazer, and yet even so Rebecca had ached for him, imagining his pain and loss.

It had been then that she had been most hopeful that he would somehow or other divine the truth...that he would appear on her doorstep abject with apology and remorse, begging her to allow him to make it up to her.

She had been very young then, too young to see that Frazer had never really shared her deep, almost compulsive need to preserve their friendship, but then Frazer was not in love with her as she was with him; their friendship had never meant to him what it did to her, and so gradually she had come to accept that, even if he did learn the truth, it would make very little difference.

Now a new dimension was added to that knowledge: the awareness that for some reason Frazer seemed to positively enjoy holding her at a distance.

She moved restlessly in the bed, struggling to cough as she felt her chest tighten, cursing fate as she acknowledged that it was going to be several days before she was well enough to leave.

She comforted herself with the knowledge that Frazer was hardly likely to see her out during that time and that, if she was careful and exercised every particle of her imagination, it might almost be possible for her to pretend that he wasn't in the house at all, but still safely in America.

Unfortunately this admirable plan received a severe setback in the early hours of the morning when she woke from a restless sleep, aching from head to foot, her body slick with a feverish sweat, her chest ominously tight.

Someone had thoughtfully opened the windows to their fullest extent so that she could breathe in the clear pure mountain air, but as she turned to do so she saw the low shape of the camp bed on the floor between her and the windows.

Someone was lying on it, and her heart gave a confused, shattering leap as she realised it was Frazer. Frazer sleeping here in her room...but why?

In her shock she sat up, then shivered as the night air touched her overheated skin. Her shivers brought on an increase in the tightness of her chest, making her cough and then gasp as the all too familiar pain gripped her.

Instantly Frazer was awake, but this time she managed to control the agonising spasm before he reached her.

As soon as she could speak, she demanded fiercely, 'What are you doing in here?'

'Maud was worried about you. She felt someone should be with you.' He gave a dispassionate shrug. 'She was determined enough to do it herself, so I really had no option but to offer my services instead.'

He was standing beside her bed, making her feel

ridiculously self-conscious, despite the residue of
pain still lurking threateningly in her chest.

The pyjama bottoms he was wearing were obviously not his own, flannelette and voluminous, the
legs too short despite the fact that the waist had
dropped to his hips. Uncomfortably Rebecca was
aware that, since she was lying facing him and he
was standing up, unless she turned on to her other
side or closed her eyes there was no way she could
avoid the sight of his bare torso and flat, hard belly.

The dark line of hair that disappeared under the
knotted cord of his borrowed pyjamas was causing
the oddest sensations to gather ominously in the pit
of her own stomach, sensations so intense that she
instinctively slid her hand beneath the bedcovers
and placed her palm firmly against her stomach as
though to suppress them before giving in to the
cowardly impulse to turn on to her other side and
hope that he would go away.

He didn't. Instead, shockingly, she felt the hard
warmth of his palm on the cold flesh of her back,
the firm stimulation of his hand not only rubbing
away the cold but also easing the nagging pain from
her tormented lungs.

Dizzily she wondered how he had known just
how much she had needed to feel the comforting
heat melting away her pain, and as though in an-

swer he said quietly, 'I had pneumonia once myself. Not very pleasant.'

'No,' Rebecca agreed shortly. She was having difficulty breathing, never mind speaking, and her difficulty had nothing at all to do with her illness. The sensation of his hard male palm moving rhythmically against her skin was doing far more than merely alleviating the pain in her lungs. The heat from the unexpected contact had spread right through her entire body, sending up a shocking frisson of sensation from the pit of her stomach.

All too uncomfortably conscious of the way her body was reacting to him and praying that he wouldn't notice and start asking questions she could not answer, she was caught off guard when he invited casually, 'Tell me again what you were doing in the mill pond.'

What she was doing? Baffled, she focused on him, forgetting the dangers of doing so.

It had been a long time since she had been as close to him as this. The last time...the last time must have been the day of her eighteenth birthday, when he had kissed her...not as she had longed for him to kiss her in her fevered adolescent dreams, but not quite either, surely, in a way that was totally non-sexual.

Then, though, they had both been fully dressed, and she had not been anything like as aware of her own sensuality and needs. Abruptly she tried to focus on his question.

'You know what I was doing. Peter's jacket...'

There was a pause. Frazer's hand was removed, and shockingly his hands were on her upper arms, turning her to face him.

'Liar,' he said calmly 'It wasn't Peter's *jacket* that took you into the water at all, was it? It was the fact that you thought *Peter* was inside it.'

Her face gave her away, even before she whispered betrayingly, 'How did you guess?'

'I didn't,' he told her curtly, his expression darkening. 'The twins told me. They hadn't realised until I arrived on the scene just what danger you were in. They'd been so subdued all evening, I guessed something was going on. When I tackled them about it they told me the truth.'

All of it? Rebecca wondered, then got her answer when Frazer continued grimly, 'I've made sure that they're now fully aware of the dangers of playing that kind of game, and that, while it might originally have seemed a good idea to tease you by pretending Peter had fallen in the water, it could have resulted in terrible tragedy.'

'Did they tell you *why* they were teasing me?' Rebecca asked him, deliberately pulling free of his hold and looking away from him.

'Oh, apparently they got impatient because you were late joining them.'

So they hadn't told him! She had suspected not. After all, they must both have realised by now, after hearing the way Frazer reacted to her, that they need have no fears that she was going to come between them.

'It's a pity that Maud saw fit to dismiss Carole. Maud thinks they ought to be sent to boarding school.'

'No!' Rebecca interrupted him vehemently, surprising herself as much as she obviously had him. He was frowning at her, and yet at the same time there was a look in his eyes that made her heart thud uncomfortably.

'So protective of them. Why? Or can I guess? They're Rory's children, therefore...'

'That has nothing to do with it,' Rebecca denied angrily. 'The twins are obviously insecure and afraid. That's what makes them react the way they do. They're constantly testing the adults around them, searching for proof that they're loved and wanted. If you send them away they'll interpret that as another rejection. It's bad enough that they hardly ever see their parents.'

'You and Robert attending boarding schools,' Frazer pointed out.

'Robert and I knew that our parents loved us.

They were very careful to explain why it was necessary for them to be away, and when they did come home they made sure that we knew how much they loved us. Peter and Helen haven't mentioned their parents once since I've been here. They've talked about you...' She bit her lip, remembering how sometimes she wished they would not, because even hearing the sound of his name had the power to hurt her, especially now that she was here living in his home.

She saw that Frazer was frowning.

'You sound very convincing.'

'Children are my job,' she reminded him tiredly. 'Which was why Aunt Maud rang me and asked me to come up here.'

'Is it?' The dry tone of his voice and the way he looked at her made her skin burn.

Half of her wanted to challenge him and ask what other possible reason there could be, but she didn't have the courage, so she said jerkily instead, 'I warned her that you wouldn't want me here, but...' She shivered suddenly and saw his frown deepen.

'Stop talking and go back to sleep. I don't want the doctor accusing me of neglecting you to such an extent that you're getting worse and not better.'

'No,' she agreed wryly. 'The sooner I'm better and able to leave, the happier you'll be. I'm well aware of that fact, Frazer.'

She lay down and started to pull the bedclothes up around her, tensing when her fingers tangled with Frazer's and were pushed unceremoniously out of the way as he took the covers from her and firmly and efficiently tucked them round her.

As he saw the astonishment widening her eyes, he reminded her drolly, 'You're not the only one with parenting experience, you know.'

And then, just as he was about to move away, he added in a completely different tone, 'I suppose I have to thank the fact that you're not well for your amazing self-denial in not reminding me that I now owe you an apology. I had no idea that you actually thought it was Peter in the pool. Why didn't you tell me?'

Gravely Rebecca met the look he was giving her and said quietly, 'There didn't seem much point.'

It was silly that, where she should have felt triumph, all she *could* feel was a sudden painful sadness and an aching wish that it was somehow possible for them to wipe out the last few years and start again.

CHAPTER FIVE

'SHUSH! Uncle Frazer said we weren't to wake her up!'

Reluctantly Rebecca opened her eyes. The twins were standing beside her bed staring down at her, and her glance was drawn past them to the narrow camp bed where Frazer had spent the night. Her heart thumped erratically, her emotions and senses affected by the memory of him.

'Aunt Maud says that you're very poorly and that you mustn't be disturbed,' Peter informed her, staring curiously at her.

'And *I* said, I think, that you two weren't to come up here and wake Rebecca up,' said Frazer from the door.

Three pairs of eyes swivelled in his direction, all of them betraying varying degrees of guilt. The twins' he could understand. Rebecca's... Uncomfortably he acknowledged that it was no one's fault but his own, if she looked at him with the same half nervous, half resentful wariness of her much younger relatives.

In the past he had had good reason for acting the way he had, but yesterday...

'Downstairs, you two,' he commanded, but Rebecca shook her head and said, 'Let them stay.'

Let them stay, because that way they'll be a barrier between us, was what she was really saying, and both of them knew it.

'I could read you a story if you like,' offered Peter, obviously determined to make amends for past misdemeanours. 'Uncle Frazer always reads to me when I don't feel well. I like it best when he sits in the big chair in our room and we sit on his knee.'

Rebecca would have given everything she owned and then some more not to be looking at Frazer at that particular moment. She had a brief and all too illuminating mental image of the chair in question, and of herself and not the twins curled up against the hard warmth of Frazer's body. She blinked desperately to banish the tormenting image, then flushed scarlet as she saw the way Frazer was looking at her.

'Rebecca can't sit on Frazer's knee, she's too big,' Helen was saying scornfully to her brother, creating a much-needed diversion, although Rebecca could have wished she had chosen a much less dangerous topic.

'And besides, it's the very last place you'd

choose to be, isn't it?' Frazer murmured to her, while the twins argued. 'Now if I were Rory…'

It was odd that relief could make her feel so flat and sharp with disappointment.

'Well, you aren't, are you?' she said acidly. Was he really so blind? Did he honestly not know how she felt about him? She ought to have been glad, but instead she felt angry and hurt, which was ridiculous. The last thing she wanted was for him to guess how she really felt.

THE TWINS spent most of the morning with her. The knowledge that she had not betrayed them to Frazer seemed to have broken down some of the barriers between them, although Rebecca knew that both of them were still wary with her.

When the doctor came he frowned and announced that the congestion on her lungs was not showing any sign of improvement, but when she protested that she was feeling fine and that the last thing she needed was to spend more time in bed, he agreed that she could get up, but warned her that she was not to attempt to do anything more than sit quietly in a warm room; and when she tentatively mentioned the possibility of travelling home, he was horrified.

It was unfortunate that Frazer should knock on her door and walk in just as the doctor was explaining to her that it was impossible for her to even think of travelling home for at least a week. He frowned as he listened to the conversation, then when the doctor had finished said coolly, 'I'm afraid Rebecca is used to a far more exciting life than we lead up here...hence her urgent desire to return to London.'

She waited until the doctor had gone before hissing at him, 'You know very well the only reason I want to go back is that I know how much you hate having me here!'

'The only reason...' Frazer's eyebrows rose. 'What about these impetuous male admirers of yours we hear so many reports of? Your mother's letters to Maud are full of constant references to your social popularity. Maud complains that she barely sees the same man's name twice in your mother's accounts of your affairs.'

Rebecca glowered at him, wondering if his use of the word affair was deliberate, and mentally cursing her mother, who had obviously very valiantly indulged in a maternally defensive embroidery exercise of the truth.

'Frazer...what did the doctor say?' Aunt Maud came in, looking worried. 'I saw him on his way out and he says that Rebecca isn't any better.'

'Yes, I am,' Rebecca lied. 'He told me I could

get up and go downstairs, and I'm sure that by to-morrow I'll be well enough to leave.'

'Rubbish! You're not going anywhere, my girl, until *I'm* convinced that you're well enough to do so!'

The sharp pronouncement stunned Rebecca, until she realised that Frazer, with his strong sense of family and duty, was probably thinking of her parents and their feelings if they discovered that their daughter had been allowed to return home before she was fully recovered. His concern certainly couldn't contain anything personal...any fears for her as an individual.

She wanted to tell him that she would leave when she chose, but Aunt Maud was already fussing round her, telling her she looked far too thin and frail, saying they would light the sitting-room fire and that she could sit there once the room was properly warm.

Despite the fact that Frazer did not approve, or perhaps because of it, Rebecca secretly admitted, she insisted on getting up to join the rest of the family for lunch. When Frazer told her grimly that she was being a fool, she tilted her chin and said defiantly, 'I feel perfectly well enough to get up, Frazer,' then added dangerously and untruthfully, 'So well, in fact, that I'm sure I'll be able to go home tomorrow.'

'Liar,' Frazer said unemotionally. 'If you feel anything like the way you look, and I suspect you do, you'd be doing exactly what the doctor wants you to do and staying right here in bed.'

Rebelliously Rebecca refused to listen either to him or to her own awareness of her body's vulnerability. She had stubbornly refused to accept her own doctor's warning earlier in the year and had suffered the consequences, but this time it was different, she argued; this time she was nowhere near as ill.

But neither was she completely well, as she discovered over lunch. Frazer had offered to carry her downstairs, but she had grimly refused his offer of assistance.

Now the twins' chatter was making her head ache; her throat felt sore and dry, and she suspected that on top of everything else she was well on the way to having an appalling head cold.

She was frankly relieved when, after lunch, Frazer announced that he had work to do and took himself off to his study.

'I don't know why he hasn't gone back to the States,' Rebecca grumbled to Aunt Maud, for once letting her guard down, as the older woman kept her company in front of the sitting-room fire.

Despite the fact that it was summer, the stone-walled house was cool enough inside to merit the luxury of lighting the fire. Aunt Maud had never been totally convinced that central heating was beneficial to one's health, so the radiators at Aysgarth were very rarely more than lukewarm, and today Rebecca was very conscious of the chilliness of the old house.

'There wouldn't be any point, my dear. The tour has been cancelled. Privately, I suspect Frazer was never very keen on the idea in the first place. You know how he feels about the Institute. I suspect he believes the place would collapse without him. Men!'

'Well, if he feels like that, why doesn't he go there?' Rebecca muttered under her breath, forgetting that Aunt Maud could have remarkably sharp ears when it suited her.

'Rebecca, how can he?' Aunt Maud reproached. 'When he's so worried about you! If he hadn't arrived when he did…' She gave a shudder that for once wasn't theatrical, suddenly looking very old and surprisingly frail for such a vigorous person. 'What on earth should I have said to your parents? When I think of what those appalling children tried to do.' She fixed a stern stare on Rebecca when Rebecca tried to interrupt her and said fiercely, 'And don't try to convince me that they didn't realise your danger. Frazer might choose to believe that, but I'm far from convinced. I've said it before and I shall say it again: the pair of them should be at boarding school. Either that or Frazer will have to find himself a wife to take proper charge of them. It's all very well Rory saying that they're better off here with Frazer, but Frazer has his own life to lead. If he shouldn't decide to marry...'

If... Rebecca licked suddenly dry lips, aching to ask her great-aunt if she suspected that Frazer might in actual fact be involved enough with someone to be thinking of marriage, and yet terrified of doing so. Even now, when she knew how hopeless her own feelings were, she couldn't bear to hear that Frazer loved someone else. How ridiculous! Her feelings were more suitable for a teenager than a grown woman.

'You've gone very pale, dear. Perhaps a cup of tea?' Aunt Maud suggested solicitously, which was how Rebecca came to be on her own when the sitting-room door opened, and a familiar voice exclaimed, 'Rebecca, my very favourite second cousin! What on earth are you doing here? Don't say my dear brother has relented at long last and admitted you back into the fold?'

And then she was being dragged to her feet and kissed provocatively on the mouth by Rory, while she struggled to protest both at his far from fraternal kiss, and at the unexpected shock of seeing him.

She was still in his arms when the twins suddenly

burst into the room, followed by Frazer, and Rebecca was mortified by the contemptuous look Frazer gave her.

How could she protest that it was not her fault, that Rory had taken her off guard, and that his flirtatious and possessive manner towards her was, she was sure, designed purely and simply to annoy his elder brother?

'How very thoughtful of you, dear brother, to arrange for my favourite cousin to be here to welcome me!'

Had Rory always been so ready to taunt Frazer? Rebecca had never noticed it before, but she had been too young then to be aware of the undercurrents in people's relationships. She had seen them simply as brothers, and of the two of them, her attention had always been focused more on Frazer than Rory.

'What are *you* doing here, Rory?' Frazer demanded curtly, ignoring his comment.

'I had to come to London for a head office interview for a new promotion. So we thought we'd see how the brats were doing.' Rory's eyes narrowed mockingly. 'Don't tell me that I'm not welcome?'

'*We?*' Frazer pressed.

'Yes. Lillian stopped off in London to see her parents. She'll be joining me up here tomorrow. She seemed to think it was time we checked up on these two,' Rory added airily, indicating the silent and almost hostile twins, who, Rebecca had noticed, had crept closer to Frazer.

Inside she wept for them, and wondered why she had never realised before that Rory was cruel as well as shallow. Couldn't he see how much he was damaging them with his careless and uncaring attitude towards them? She remembered how when her own parents used to come home her father had swept both her and Robert into his arms, hugging them fiercely, letting them know how much they were missed and loved.

Rory had made no attempt to touch his children, and was still standing next to her, his hand resting possessively on her shoulder, his fingers stroking her skin. A tiny shudder of revulsion went through her, and she gritted her teeth against it.

'I was just saying to Rebecca that it's a surprise to see her here. I thought she was still forbidden the place.' Rory laughed in amusement. 'Mind you, I'm glad she is here. We'll be able to spend some time together while Lillian does her doting mother bit.'

Rebecca couldn't say a word. She was too stunned by Rory's appalling selfishness. Didn't he care that the twins were there listening to what he was saying? Had he really no conception of what he was doing to them?

She was too caught up in her anger on the twins' behalf to pay much attention to what Frazer was saying until she caught her own name and focused on him just in time to hear him announced, shockingly, 'I'm afraid Rebecca won't be able to spend her time keeping you amused, Rory.'

She waited for him to explain that she was being packed off home, but Rory challenged smoothly and softly, 'Isn't that for Rebecca to say, Frazer? As I remember, she once used to enjoy my company very much indeed.'

The sheer audacity of it took Rebecca's breath away. There had never been the kind of relationship between them that Rory was intimating, and once she was alone with him she intended to demand to know what he thought he was doing in suggesting that there had. All right, so he wanted to annoy Frazer...but she was not going to be dragged into their quarrels.

'Once, maybe,' Frazer agreed urbanely. 'But now she and I are engaged...'

'*Engaged!*' Rebecca's own whispered repetition of the word was lost beneath Rory's louder, almost angry, 'You and Rebecca engaged? Since when? You've always hated the sight of one another!'

There was a moment's pause while Rebecca tried

to deal with the pain flowering inside her and declare that Frazer was lying, but by the time she had the pain under control it was too late, and Frazer was saying quietly, and with such conviction that she felt herself quiver inside with unwanted emotion, 'Once, maybe, but we've learned better now. Haven't we, my love?'

She could only stare at him in disbelief as he came to her side and took hold of her hand, lifting it to his mouth. His lips were warm and firm against her skin, but his eyes were icy cold, warning her not to deny what he was saying.

Of course Aunt Maud would choose that moment to arrive with Mrs Norton and the tea tray, and of course Rory would barely allow her to get over the shock of seeing him before saying queryingly, 'I gather I'm not the only surprise you've been having,' then he turned to Frazer and asked directly, 'Rebecca isn't wearing a ring, Frazer. How long *have* you been engaged?'

'Since this morning,' Frazer lied promptly, 'or rather, since last night.' The look he gave her made Rebecca go scarlet, as much with indignation as with shock. 'I think it must have been the catalyst of almost losing her that brought me to my senses, and made me realise exactly how I feel about her.'

There was a moment's silence, then Rory looked at her and said unkindly, 'And you, of course, Rebecca, have always had a weakness for my big brother, haven't you? How very unfortunate that I should choose to arrive so untimely, like a spectre at the feast, stirring up unwanted memories! You're a very lucky man, Frazer—as I have good reason to know.'

Rebecca could only stare at him, her shock at Frazer's unexpected announcement superseded as she wondered why she had never seen this malice in Rory before. Had she and Frazer really been in love and engaged, how very painful it would have been for both of them to be reminded that supposedly she had loved the other brother first, and loved him recklessly and foolishly enough to break his marriage vows with him.

'So,' Rory asked suavely surveying their silent faces, 'when is the wedding to be?'

It was Aunt Maud who answered, saying briskly, 'As soon as Rebecca's parents return from Australia, of course.' Rebecca stared at her. Surely Aunt Maud didn't really believe they were engaged? She must realise…but apparently she didn't, because she was saying firmly to Rory, 'I think it might be an idea if you spent time with your children, Rory. They could certainly do with some supervision,' she added curtly.

LATER IT SEEMED to Rebecca that days and not hours passed before she was finally able to see Fra-

zer on his own and tackle him about his incredible
announcement.

In the end it was Maud who gave her the opening
she needed. Having exhausted the topic of the wedding she had now virtually planned down to the last
detail, she suddenly announced unexpectedly that
Rebecca looked tired and that they must none of
them forget how very lucky they were that she was
still with them at all. This, accompanied by a dark
look at the twins, had Rebecca sighing faintly and
wishing that Aunt Maud could be a little more tact-
ful and a little less forthright, but when she added
firmly, 'Frazer, I think you'd better help Rebecca
upstairs,' she reflected that such forthrightness had
its advantages after all.

Rory raised one eyebrow and said drolly, 'My
dear Maud, is that wise—allowing them to be
alone? Perhaps I ought to go with them as chape-
ron.'

'Thank you, Rory, but that won't be necessary,'
Frazer said calmly.

As she hobbled towards the door, Rebecca wondered if anyone else beside herself had been aware
of the edge of malice creeping up under Rory's apparently teasing comment.

Now more than ever, she wished it were possible
for her to go home. It had been bad enough antic-

ipating spending close on another week here when she had had Frazer's antipathy towards her to contend with, but now, with Rory here as well...

She gave a small shudder, unaware that Frazer was watching her as he held the door open for her, until he said sharply, 'You're cold.'

'No, not really...'

Something in her expression must have betrayed what she was thinking, because as he guided her towards the stairs Frazer said harshly, 'You've only yourself to blame, you know. It's never wise to put people on pedestals. When they're revealed as mere human beings, it can be a painful process, but then I should have thought you'd already realised that my brother enjoys hurting people. He's jealous, of course.'

'Jealous?' Rebecca stopped and stared at him. 'Don't be ridiculous! How can he be?' and then she stopped, realising that what Frazer said was true, and that Rory *was* jealous of his older brother. Had that jealousy always been there, and had she been too naïve and inexperienced to see it? But if it had, surely Rory would not have begged her to pretend that they had had an affair? Surely he would have delighted in revealing to Frazer that he and she had been lovers? Or perhaps he had not dared risk revealing the truth.

Because this afternoon, she had realised something else. Rory might be jealous of his older brother, but he was also just a little in awe of him.

She raised her head and saw that Frazer was looking at her, giving her a mocking, unkind look that made her body tense uneasily.

'Why? I should have thought that was obvious. I now have something he believes he wants.'

It took a moment for his meaning to sink in, and when it did Rebecca said furiously, 'Is *that* why you said we were engaged? Because you think *Rory* wants me?' All her pent-up feelings of anger and disgust were in her voice. 'I've thought you many things over the years, Frazer, most of them uncomplimentary, but I've never thought of you as being petty or vengeful—and besides, you're wrong. Rory *doesn't* want me at all,' she told him scornfully. 'In fact...'

She stopped abruptly, realising that she was on the edge of admitting the truth.

'No, *you're* the one who's wrong,' Frazer told her grimly. 'I saw the way he was looking at you—and you can disabuse your mind of its infantile belief that my announcement of our engagement was motivated by petty fraternal and juvenile emotions. Eight years ago, I told you that Rory was a married man. He still is. He still has those same responsibilities now that he had then. You heard what he said—he and Lillian have come here to spend some time with the children, and if you think I'm going to let your presence here damage their marriage by allowing you and Rory to indulge in some romantic dream of might-have-beens, then you can think again. Because I'm not. That's why I told him we were engaged.'

Rebecca stared at him, lost for words. Did he really think she posed that kind of threat to Rory's marriage? If so, it must be a very fragile structure indeed.

'You're out of your mind!' she told him grimly when she could speak. 'To go to such lengths! All you needed to do was to let me leave…'

'And have Rory come haring after you? Is that what you had in mind? A passionate reunion, somewhere private where the two of you could be alone?'

His voice had dropped to ice-cold derision, and Rebecca shivered under the contemptuous lash of it. What he was saying was so far from the truth that it was risible, but the last thing she felt like doing was laughing.

Frazer saw her shiver and said curtly, 'You're frozen.'

He was walking towards her and had just reached her when the sitting-room door opened and Rory emerged, looking bored and irritated. When he saw them, he smiled tauntingly.

'Still here? Very slow of you, brother dear! In your shoes, I'd have lost no time in whisking Rebecca upstairs to the privacy of her room.'

Rebecca stiffened angrily. She had been used once by Rory in his jealousy against his brother; she was not going to allow herself to be used again.

She started to move away from Frazer, intent on leaving them alone, when suddenly she found that she couldn't move and that the solid wall of his chest was in front of her while somehow or other his arms had locked round her body.

The only advantage of the situation was the fact that the bulk of Frazer's body hid her from Rory's view, and that advantage was heavily outweighed by all the disadvantages of her unwelcome position, which included the knowledge that her heart had started to pound at a startlingly fast rate and that her body was reacting nervously and very betrayingly to the proximity of Frazer's.

In a voice she barely recognised as belonging to the Frazer she knew, so soft and thickened was it, she heard him saying rawly, 'Go away, Rory.'

And then somehow or other his hand was cupping her face, firmly holding her so that she couldn't turn away from the downward descent of his mouth. She caught a momentary glimpse of his eyes, feral and dark, cold no longer, but startlingly quicksilver with heat. Her lips parted on an instinc-

tive protest, but the sound was silenced by the firm
pressure of his mouth. She sagged weakly against
him, shivering with shock and anger that he should
treat her like this.

Rory was still there, watching them. Rebecca
could sense his presence without looking at him,
and it crossed her mind that if she and Rory had
actually been lovers, then his demonstration that
Frazer was patently staging for his benefit was
hardly conducive to restoring good family relations.

She tried to hold on to that thought as Frazer
continued to kiss her. His hand had left her face
now and was buried in her hair, the pressure of his
mouth against hers forcing her back against his
other arm. Beneath her weakness and shock, heat
ran like liquid fire through her veins, the fine trembling of her body no longer caused by anger. The
sensation of Frazer's hand moving to the small of
her back, caressing her, burned through the fragile
protection of her clothes.

He moved slightly, moving her with him, so that
their movement caused the fabrics of their clothes
to rustle provocatively together, and then she felt
the hard pressure of his leg pushing against her
body as he subtly used his greater strength to ma-
noeuvre her so that she had no option but to accept
the visually erotic embrace. Her hands were already
clinging to his shoulders, although she had no

knowledge of putting them there, and, when she tried to protest at his actions beneath the pressure of his mouth, his teeth nipped punishingly at her lower lip and then his tongue caressed the bruised tender flesh, causing such a fierce flood of sensation to pour through her that if Rory hadn't slammed the sitting-room door, shocking her back to reality, she would not have been able to stop the small moan building in her throat; a sound that had nothing at all to do with any physical discomfort from the sharp pressure of Frazer's teeth, raking the soft inner tenderness of her lip, and everything to do with the shockingly pleasurable sensations that caress had aroused.

He let her go almost abruptly; too abruptly for her to be able to conceal from him the stunned, almost bruised expression in her eyes.

Instinctively she lifted her hand to her mouth, and for a second something primitive and dangerous blazed in the dark heat of Frazer's eyes.

'You can't do this!' Rebecca whispered painfully. 'No one is going to believe that we're engaged. Everyone will realise what you're doing.'

'I don't give a damn what everyone else thinks, just so long as Rory believes it, and if *you* give him any reason to believe otherwise, I'll make you sorrier than you can think possible. I suppose you believe you still love him,' he added broodingly.

Here was her chance to escape, and all she had to do was to tell the truth.

She shook her head and said firmly, 'No, I don't.'

For a moment it was almost as though what she said had shocked him. She could almost feel a totally unexpected tension emanating from him, and when she looked closely at him she saw a brief flicker of emotion disturb his otherwise impassive features. He looked if anything almost angry, and yet why the knowledge that she did not love Rory should make him angry she had no idea. Rather she would have thought the news would have pleased him. Irritating, aggravating man! He never seemed to react as she expected. By rights she ought to walk away from him right now and leave him to explain to everyone just how he lied to them, but she knew that she wouldn't...couldn't...

'All I want is to leave this house and go back to London. If you hadn't said we were engaged, I could have done that,' she told him fiercely.

'And have Rory follow you down there? No, you're safer here where I can keep an eye on you...where I can make sure that he knows that you're out of bounds.'

'Has it occurred to you that the fact that he believes I'm engaged to you might increase my appeal rather than diminish it?' Rebecca asked him tartly.

'Maybe so, but Lillian will be here in a few days

and between us I'm sure that she and I can make sure he realises he'd be wasting his time. You say you don't love him. Prove it,' Frazer ordered unexpectedly.

'By doing what? Letting everyone believe that we're engaged? I can't. Aunt Maud…'

'I'll talk to her,' he told her. 'If it's your parents you're worried about, I'll make sure she understands the real reason for what I said.'

'It's crazy!' Rebecca protested. 'It would be so much simpler if you just let me leave.'

'Do you honestly believe that would be enough?' he demanded bitterly. 'I saw the way Rory was looking at you.'

'But I'll be leaving anyway in a week.'

'Why?' he asked her baldly, silencing her. 'You don't have to go back to London, do you? After all, you'd already made a commitment to stay here until September.'

'But you *wanted* me to leave,' she protested Her mind seemed to have turned to cotton wool again, and, although she knew there must be a hundred or more excellent reasons why she should stand firm and tell Frazer that there was no way she was going to allow him to manipulate her like this, she couldn't summon one strong enough to convince herself, never mind him.

He gave her a cynical look and asked acidly:

'Since when have my wishes been so important to you? Think of the twins, Rebecca. You said yourself that they needed a stable background and proper family life. You wanted to help them…well, here's your chance. The best way you can help them is by keeping their parents' marriage intact.'

Rebecca knew what he said was true. To adult eyes, Rory and Lillian might not have a very good marriage, but children were blind to the faults in their parents' relationships. As she knew from experience, it would be far more important in the twins' eyes that their parents remained together. Children hated their parents divorcing, and these two were more vulnerable than most.

She felt dreadfully tired, her mind and body aching with the strain of the last few days, and as she nodded bleakly she had the uncomfortable conviction that she was doing the wrong thing, but it was already too late. Frazer was already saying curtly, 'Right then, we're agreed. You and I are now engaged.'

'Temporarily,' Rebecca added tiredly, turning to go upstairs.

'But of course,' he agreed urbanely. 'How could it be anything else?'

How indeed? Foolish of her to make that rider. After all, she knew quite well that Frazer would be only too glad when the time came for him to dismiss her from his life.

CHAPTER SIX

WHEN she opened her eyes in the morning, Rebecca cravenly contemplated suffering a relapse of sufficiently dramatic proportions to ensure her prompt removal somewhere safe and calm, like the nearest hospital, but it only took a very few seconds' contemplation of this proposal for her to acknowledge its shortcomings.

It was true that she did still feel very weak and that her chest still hurt, but she was far more anxious about how on earth she was going to survive the next few weeks than she was about her health.

She could only hope and pray that Rory got bored with life at Aysgarth and took himself and his family away from it at the earliest opportunity. Only then would she be free to escape from Frazer and go on with her own life.

Odd to think how once she had dreamed of this—being engaged to Frazer. But not this kind of engagement, of course—a proper one, all hearts and flowers, ring and promises...all the things that girls of eighteen did dream of. But she wasn't eighteen any more, and those dreams had been as fictional as her present engagement.

She sat up in bed, wincing as she felt a sharp reminding pain grip her chest. She might claim to Frazer that she felt well enough to leave, but she knew that in reality she wasn't. She had been far more ill earlier in the year than she was prepared to admit to anyone other than her own doctor and her mother, and all through her own dangerous neglect of her health. She had no wish to feel like that ever again. Besides, it was pointless now thinking of excuses to leave. She was committed, and Frazer would make sure she stood by that commitment.

Her bedroom door opened and she tensed, half expecting Frazer to walk in, mentally preparing herself for the sharply painful pleasure of seeing him, but it was Helen who walked into her bedroom.

The unexpected sight of the little girl, for once without her faithful shadow Peter, took Rebecca rather aback.

'Is it true that you and Frazer are going to get married?' Helen demanded aggressively.

Rebecca felt her heart drop. She ought to have been prepared for this; after all, she knew how the twins, especially Helen, felt about Frazer, but somehow or other she had been too caught up in her own feelings and reactions to give more than a cursory thought to theirs.

She toyed with the idea of telling Helen the truth, then reluctantly decided that she couldn't. The little girl was too young to understand the reasons for Frazer's deception—then she reminded herself hardily that, since it was Frazer who was promoting the importance of Rory and Lillian's marriage, it was he who could deal with the little girl's obvious resentment of their 'engagement.'

'Yes,' she admitted, and then because at heart she couldn't bear to hurt anyone, especially not this outwardly aggressive but inwardly so vulnerable child, she added quietly, 'But that won't make any difference to the very special place that you and Peter have in Frazer's life, Helen.'

Scornful hazel eyes studied her.

'Of course it will! You'll make Frazer send us away to school, and you'll have babies and...'

How well she understood the feelings motivating the child, Rebecca thought wryly, looking at the now downbent head, and suspecting that tears were already darkening the hazel eyes. Tears which Helen didn't want her to see. Impossible to cuddle and console this prickly little creature...impossible to do anything other than tactfully look the other way while she battled with her emotions.

Both of them were taken by surprise when Frazer *did* walk in through the open door, frowning a querying look at Rebecca over Helen's downbent head and asking crisply, 'What's wrong?'

'Helen's worried that when you and I get married, I'll make you send her and Peter away to school,' Rebecca told him sharply, in a 'now see what you've done!' voice.

She knew from the look Frazer gave her that he had picked up her unsubtle message, and she knew also that she had widened the rift between herself and Helen, when the little girl's head came up and she said belligerently, 'I know you want us to go away. Daddy told us last night that you wouldn't want us here now.'

Oh, yes, she could well imagine Rory saying that. How could he be so selfish and thoughtless? How could he hurt his own children simply out of his need to get at Frazer?

While Rebecca was thinking this, she heard Frazer saying grimly, 'I own Aysgarth, Helen, not your father, and I promise you that you and Peter will always have a place here.'

'Even when you marry *her*?' demanded Helen, ignoring Rebecca and scuffing one foot on the carpet, her head still downbent, her voice truculent, but under the truculence a note of almost despairing pleading for reassurance.

Rebecca ached for her. How could Rory and Lillian do this to their children? Couldn't they *see* how much they needed them? It was wrong that Frazer should have to supply the love and emotional support the twins should have received from their parents, no matter how willingly he might give it.

'*Especially* once Rebecca and I are married,' Frazer said firmly, and then, to Rebecca's surprise, he came over to the bed and reached down to lift her hand off the covers, holding it firmly in his own, so that his thumb brushed against the pulse in her inner wrist and she was immediately aware of the warmth and strength emanating from him. His free hand he held out to Helen, and astonishingly, to Rebecca at least, the little girl walked over to him, allowing him to draw her into the circle of his arm.

'Rebecca and I both promise you that you and Peter will always have a home here, don't we, Rebecca?'

As solemnly as though she were swearing an oath on the Bible, Rebecca said softly, 'Yes, we do.'

Her fears and antipathy were forgotten in the importance of Helen's need. Nothing right now was more important than sharing with Frazer the need to reassure her, to make her know that she would always have her own special place here, and she badly needed that knowledge, Rebecca knew.

From the shelter of Frazer's arm, Helen asked

warily, 'But what about when you and Rebecca have babies?'

There was a small pause, and Rebecca wondered if she had merely imagined the sudden clenching of the hand that held her own. Certainly she was not imagining the rapid increase in her own pulse rate, the shallow, nervous tenor of her breathing as she reacted with unexpected intensity to the lure of those innocent words.

A child...Frazer's child. Her body ached and tightened as though it already knew how it would feel to have that child growing inside her.

She forced herself to dismiss her feelings and to concentrate instead on what Frazer was saying.

'Well then, they're going to need your help to get to know all about living at Aysgarth—and that doesn't include teaching them to throw expensive anoraks into the millpond,' Frazer added mock-severely. 'It doesn't matter how many children Rebecca and I have, Helen, we won't stop loving you,' he told the little girl gently.

When Helen burst into tears and hid her head against Frazer's chest, Rebecca herself wasn't all that far away from feeling weepy. Frazer would make a wonderful father; he seemed to know instinctively how to react to a child's needs.

It was only when Helen had gone to find Peter and impart the good news to him that Rebecca was able to say quietly, 'That's been on her mind for a long time. She's petrified of losing you.'

'All the more reason to give Rory and Lillian every encouragement to start forming a closer relationship with their children,' he said. 'I meant what I said. The twins will always have a place here, but already both of them are developing vulnerabilities and anxieties that are going to cripple them all through their lives, unless something's done about them, and soon.'

'How long will it be before Lillian arrives?' Rebecca asked him.

'I'm not sure. According to Rory she's just spending a couple of days with her parents. He says she's the one who instituted this visit, and it certainly isn't like Rory to volunteer to spend time with the children.' Frazer made an exasperated sound of irritation. 'They should never really have had a family at all. I doubt that the twins' arrival was planned, and of course Lillian is in a very invidious position; she either stays in England with the twins and risks the destruction of her marriage, or she goes with Rory, and endures the separation from her children. In her shoes, what would you choose to do, Rebecca?' he finished.

It was the first really non-aggressive question he had asked her.

'I don't know,' she admitted. 'I'd want to be with

the man I loved, of course—what woman wouldn't—but the children's needs would probably be paramount to my own. My mother stayed with us until we were both old enough to understand why Dad spent so much time abroad, and why she had to be with him.'

'Your parents took the trouble to make sure you were both emotionally secure.'

'Yes, and we certainly didn't have to live with the knowledge that they might divorce and go their separate ways.'

'And Peter and Helen do? What makes you say that? Has Rory told you that he's planning to divorce Lillian?' Frazer asked her cynically.

'No, of course not. I was just assuming that the children knew that their parents were having problems.'

'I doubt it. Children can be remarkably selective about only hearing what they want to hear.'

'So can some adults,' Rebecca muttered under her breath, then asked, 'Did you want anything specific? Because if not, perhaps you'd like to leave so that I can get dressed.'

'Nothing too specific...just this,' Frazer told her smoothly, leaning over her and capturing her mouth with his.

The unexpectedness of it gave Rebecca no chance to summon her defences. She felt Frazer's hand on her throat pushing aside the collar of her nightshirt, his fingers tracing her collarbone, before cupping the round curve of her shoulder.

She made a soft protest beneath his mouth, trying to wrench herself away. As she struggled, she felt the top buttons of her nightshirt give, and fly across the room.

'My goodness me, not the sort of thing Maud would approve of at all!' The taunting mockery of Rory's voice made Rebecca freeze. 'What an impetuous lover you are, Frazer—you didn't even bother to close the door!'

Rory walked insolently into the room, then frowned as he looked down at the floor.

'And not just impetuous,' he commented softly, 'but rough as well.' He picked up the buttons and said to Frazer's impassive back, 'It really isn't necessary, you know. *I've* always preferred my...ladies to do their own undressing, haven't I, Rebecca?'

Rebecca prayed desperately that Frazer wouldn't move. During their brief struggle the front of her nightshirt had come completely unfastened and she knew from the rough contact of his shirt against her skin just how much of her body would be exposed if he moved away now.

She felt his muscles tense as he prepared to turn round, and reached out, gripping desperately at his arms.

She saw the way he frowned as he looked into her eyes, and, unable to tell him why she didn't want him to move, she begged him silently to stay where he was.

'Get out, Rory,' Frazer said starkly, still looking at her. Rebecca released her breath in a shaky sigh as Rory obeyed the command.

Frazer waited until he heard Rory going downstairs before demanding harshly, 'Still protecting him, Rebecca? You haven't stopped loving him at all, have you?'

He was starting to pull away from her. Trembling with tension, her hands fell away. She shook her head in denial of his accusation and said huskily, 'You're wrong—I—'

'Wrong? Then why the pleading look?'

As he lifted his body from hers, Rebecca made a frantic grab for the front of her nightshirt, but Frazer stopped her, his frown deepening as he saw what she had already realised. When she struggled to push him away, the buttons on the nightshirt, which was old and well worn, had been torn off, exposing her body virtually from her throat to her waist, and if he had moved away from her while Rory was still in the room his brother would have had an uninterrupted view of her naked breasts.

Now, instead, it was Frazer who was looking down at her bared flesh, holding her hands in his so that she couldn't do anything to conceal herself from him.

'You stopped me because you didn't want him to see you like this?'

He sounded almost incredulous, and that hurt her, angering her for long enough for her to forget her embarrassment and say fiercely, 'Is that so very surprising?'

'Yes, when you've already been lovers.'

Although he was watching her, his voice had lost some of its harshness as though the focus of his attention was no longer Rory and her relationship with him. His attention was, she recognised shakily, focused on her. She took an unsteady breath and then another, unaware of the provocative lift and fall of her breasts as she fought against the dizzying sensation Frazer's concentration on her was evoking.

'Or was it not so much that you didn't want Rory to see you, rather that you didn't want him to know that you'd revealed yourself like this to me?' he suggested silkily.

Rebecca was astounded both by his suggestion and by her own reaction of pain to it, and yet despite her chaotic thoughts all she could manage to say was a husky, 'I didn't reveal myself to you! It was an accident.'

'Rory wouldn't have thought so,' Frazer told her.

Suddenly Rebecca had had enough.

'I don't care what Rory would have thought, and I don't care what you think either!' she lied angrily. 'If you can't understand that I might feel embarrassed then that's your fault and not mine.'

'Well, I certainly didn't think you were clinging to me like ivy because you wanted me in your arms,' he told her drily, then added softly, 'And as for being embarrassed...'

Shockingly, his hand brushed briefly against her skin, following the line of her open nightshirt, his knuckles grazing against her nipple for a heart-stopping second that almost paralysed her.

He frowned as he felt the ripple of sensation that convulsed her, the evidence of the effect he was having on her quite plain in the sharpness of her indrawn breath and the open hardening of her nipples. He breathed in as well, his eyes suddenly smoky dark, the silence between them heavy with tension.

Outside her window, Rebecca heard a blackbird break into song, shattering both the silence and the tension. Quickly she drew back from Frazer, pulling her nightshirt protectively across her body.

He let her go, standing up and saying curtly, 'It might be better if you stayed in bed today.'

'To keep me out of Rory's way?' she asked bitterly, but she was speaking to an empty room. Frazer had already gone.

Later, when she felt strong enough, she would examine the pain of her reactions to him, of her knowledge that nothing had really changed, that he still had the power to affect her in the most intimate and dangerous way.

Her only consolation was that at least Frazer himself seemed oblivious to her real feelings towards him.

CHAPTER SEVEN

NOT that it was much consolation. Tired of her own company, and fearing that if she spent much more time alone brooding on what had happened she was likely to go quietly mad, Rebecca got up less than an hour after Frazer and left her, justifying doing so by telling herself that it would be selfishly unfair to lie in bed pretending to be an invalid with so many people in the house. Mrs Norton was a first-class housekeeper, but she had more than enough on her plate, coping with Frazer, Aunt Maud and the twins and with the addition of two and potentially three extra people to cater, and she deserved whatever help Rebecca herself could give her.

Mrs Norton, however, didn't seem to share that view, and told Rebecca firmly that she had no right to get up from her bed, not when Frazer had expressly said that she was to remain there.

'Frazer has no jurisdiction over me,' Rebecca informed the housekeeper drily, then wished she had not been so forthright as she heard Rory saying in amusement from behind her, 'I shouldn't let your new fiancé hear you saying that if I were you. Where is he, by the way?'

Forced to admit she had no idea, she was relieved when Mrs Norton came to her rescue, announcing that Frazer had gone over to the Research Centre, but that he would be back in time for lunch.

'Shame on him, deserting you and not even telling you where he was going,' murmured Rory, taking hold of her and guiding her towards the door, saying smoothly, 'I get the impression that Norty would rather have us out of her kitchen, and besides, there's something I want to discuss with you.'

Rebecca stiffened, anticipating some very tricky questions such as why she had allowed her supposed fiancé to go on believing that the two of them had had an affair when both she and Rory knew that to be a fiction.

Ever since she had realised that Frazer fully intended to go through with his plan of pretending that they were engaged, Rebecca had been worrying about this. Surely if she and Frazer *were* supposed to be in love and on the verge of getting married, the first thing she must have told him was the truth about that fictitious affair, and yet, to judge from the fact that he had deliberately tried to cause friction between Frazer and herself this morning, Rory seemed to have accepted quite readily that they were in actual fact engaged. Men were odd crea-

tures, Rebecca decided as she followed him resign-
edly, not into the sitting-room, but the old-
fashioned and slightly shabby study-cum-library,
which she had always thought of as Frazer's private
sanctuary.

She even felt slightly uncomfortable at being in
here in his absence, as though she were in some
way trespassing.

Rory, however, did not seem to share her unease,
although she noticed that he didn't sit in the large
chair behind the old-fashioned partner's desk, but
instead took one of the two chairs either side of the
fireplace, motioning to her to take the other.

'What is it you wanted to discuss with me,
Rory?' she asked him, wondering if she had been
naïve in believing that he had fallen for Frazer's fib
about their relationship and if he had perhaps deliberately waited to get her on her own to attack
that fib, knowing that she was vulnerable and
weaker than Frazer, but to her surprise he sat forward and said seriously, 'I wanted to talk to you
about the twins. Aunt Maud is agitating for them
to be sent to boarding school.' He frowned and said
sulkily, 'She keeps on making a damned fuss about
the fact that we've left them with Frazer. With your
experience you seem by far the best person to con-
sult about where to send them.' He drew his chair
closer to her own. 'Lillian seems to have this ridic-

ulous idea that I should ask the company to give me a UK-based job, but I've told her if she wants to spend her life playing mother then she'll have to do so on her own, because there's no way I'm going to tie myself down to a mortgage and suburbia.'

For a moment Rebecca was too stunned to speak. As a child she had liked Rory well enough in a distant, half-hearted fashion; he had never been anything more to her than a second cousin and Frazer's brother; it had been on Frazer that she had focused the intensity of her adolescent emotions, but now she looked at Rory and saw him without the veiling sentiment of their growing-up years, and what she saw she didn't like.

She got up and told him firmly, 'The twins are your responsibility, Rory, and quite frankly, the only reason I could think of for sending them to boarding school would be to protect them from the emotional pain of discovering the truth about their father!'

As she prepared to leave, he reached out and took hold of her wrist in a surprisingly painful grip.

'Rebecca, wait,' he begged urgently, with far more emotion in his voice than their recent exchange had led her to believe he could feel.

She focused on him, puzzled both by his intensity and by the sudden pleasure she could see in his eyes.

She had her back to the open door, but Rory was facing it.

'Please,' he said huskily, 'let me explain.' He tugged on her wrist, as though trying to pull her down to him—almost as though he was going to kiss her, Rebecca realised in sudden angry confusion.

'Lunch is ready.'

The icy coldness of Frazer's voice silenced the words of complaint she had been about to utter. She swung round, at the same moment as Rory released her, guilt flushing her skin as she remembered Frazer telling her that she was to stay in her room, unaware of the very different interpretation he might put on her flustered apprehension until she heard Rory saying emotionally, 'Oh, God, Rebecca, I'm sorry!' and then to Frazer, 'Look, Frazer, don't jump to any conclusions. Rebecca and I go back a long way. It's only natural we should have some loose ends to tie up.'

Rebecca couldn't believe her ears. Rory's behaviour had gone beyond a joke...if that was what it was intended to be. She had thought this morning, when he taunted Frazer with is own supposed relationship with her, that he was taking pleasure in trying to hurt his elder brother, but this...this deliberate attempt to sabotage their 'engagement'...

She looked helplessly at Frazer, and found herself almost stammering, 'Rory wanted to ask my advice about boarding schools for the twins,' while Rory looked on and smiled almost boyishly, cautioning her,

'It's no use, my sweet. Somehow I don't think Big Brother is going to be convinced,' and then, before either of them could speak, he added insouciantly, 'I wonder if Mrs N. has remembered how much I like her gooseberry pie.'

He was whistling as he walked out of the room. Rebecca looked helplessly at Frazer, then said nervously, 'I know how it must have looked, but I promise you all we were talking about was the twins.'

Some of her own feeling of bewildered disbelief coloured her voice, adding a conviction to her statement she herself wasn't aware of. Frazer frowned.

'We can't discuss it now. Mrs N. has enough to do without trying to keep meals hot.'

'Yes, I know,' Rebecca agreed, stepping through the door he was holding open for her. 'I offered to give her a hand earlier, but all she would say was that you'd said I was to stay in bed. I'm not an invalid, you know, Frazer, and she has more than enough to do as it is. It wouldn't be any hardship for me to take some of the chores off her shoulders. After all, I did come here to work.'

'That work's still there,' he told her, surprising her.

'But now that Rory is here, the twins...'

'Will probably be as neglected by him as they are in his absence.'

Rebecca made a shocked sound of rejection.

'Haven't you discovered yet that fatherhood isn't exactly something Rory relishes?' he asked her caustically, and she knew from the way he said it how much his brother's lack of care for his children angered him.

Even though she shared his views, she found herself saying palliatively, 'Perhaps if Rory hadn't been so young himself when they were born...'

'You always defend him, don't you? You even defended him when he threw you to the wolves and named you as his lover. What would it take to make you see the truth about him, Rebecca? You say you don't love him.'

'I don't,' she told him quickly, wishing the words unsaid when she realised how self-betraying they might be. After all, what should it matter to her *what* Frazer believed?

LUNCH WAS A SUBDUED affair, with the twins suddenly looking very small and vulnerable as they sat huddled together, putting as much distance between themselves and their father as they could.

'When do you expect Lillian to arrive?' Frazer asked Rory when they had all finished.

'She said a couple of days.' Rory looked across the table at Rebecca and invited, 'How about coming out with me tonight, Becca? We could have dinner somewhere.'

Before she could speak, Frazer intervened, saying quietly, 'Rebecca and I already have a dinner engagement this evening.'

Immediately Aunt Maud frowned.

'You never said anything about going out this evening, Frazer.'

'I didn't know we would be until this morning. A colleague has invited Rebecca and me to have dinner with him and his wife. They're quite new to the area and I think his wife is anxious to make some local friends. It won't be anything formal,' he told Rebecca cooly, then added softly, 'Wear that blue dress if you've brought it with you—the one you were wearing the night I proposed. The one that turns your eyes the colour of wild hyacinths.'

Even the twins were listening, their eyes round with curiosity and speculation—and no wonder! Rebecca thought wrathfully, wishing her fair skin did not flush so easily.

'If you'll excuse us, Aunt Maud,' Frazer stood up and reached for Rebecca's hand, 'Rebecca and I have one or two things we need to discuss.'

Her heart sinking, Rebecca allowed him to lead her out of the room, waiting until they were out of earshot to demand angrily, 'Why did you pretend we're going out tonight?'

'I wasn't pretending. We are,' Frazer told her quietly, ignoring her anger. He paused outside the study door and looked at her. 'No, not in there. This way.'

Mutely she followed him, frowning as he headed for the stairs.

He waited for her to catch up with him, then led her along the corridor, pushing open one of the bedroom doors. She didn't realise it was *his* room until she was inside and the door was closed behind them.

Instinctively she turned back towards it, but Frazer was standing between her and the door, blocking her way.

He smiled grimly when he saw the way her skin paled and then darkened, then said grittily, 'Cut out the acting, Rebecca. You've nothing to fear. I've brought you up here simply so that we can make some uninterrupted privacy.'

'And so that Rory will assume that we're making love!' she challenged.

His eyebrows rose.

'Will he? I've already warned you that I'm not prepared to tolerate a resurgence of your affair with

him, and yet when I walked into the study earlier—
my study—it was very apparent that...'

'He took me there to discuss the twins' education,' Rebecca broke in heatedly, then frowned. 'I
don't understand him. One minute we were on the
verge of having a row because I'd told him how
selfish he is, and the next, he suddenly started be-
having as though...'

'You were lovers,' Frazer supplied with dry
irony. He looked at her for a long time, then said
quietly, 'Isn't it obvious that he's jealous?'

'Jealous? What of?'

A look crossed Frazer's face which she found
hard to define. It was almost as though in some way
her words had hurt him, then his mouth hardened
and he said curtly, 'Of me, of course. Of the fact
that you and I are engaged...of the fact that I've
supposedly taken his place in your life and in your
bed.'

For a moment Rebecca was too wrapped up in
the tingling sensation of shocked pleasure that ran
through her at the images he was conjuring up—
images that made her catch her breath and fight to
still the ache growing inside her. Frazer her
lover...but that was fantasy. Reality was this idiotic, agonising, stupid situation she had got herself
into. Reality was...

'But Rory and I were...'

She stopped abruptly, realising what she had been about to say.

'You and Rory were what?' Frazer demanded savagely. 'All washed up years ago? He doesn't seem to think so. He still wants you, Rebecca, and you know that as well as I do. If you have any compassion at all for his wife and children, you'll…'

He frowned suddenly, glancing towards the door, and then before she could stop him, he picked her up and dropped her on to his bed, following her there as she struggled to sit up, furious with indignation.

'Quiet!' he told her as she opened her mouth to give voice to her indignation. 'I think that's Rory outside.'

'Rory?' Her heart started to thump uncomfortably as she remembered how Rory had interrupted them this morning; she shivered a little, her eyes darkening with apprehension as she stared fixedly at the door.

She could hear Rory whistling, and held her breath, her stomach muscles tensing, expecting him to come walking in.

'Rebecca.'

She turned her head automatically at the sound of Frazer's voice, her eyes widening as she realised how close to her he was. Close enough for her to see the rough graining of his skin; close enough for her to reach out and touch him if she wished, to run her fingertips along the line of shaved skin that was already beginning to darken slightly.

Her throat had gone dry; a tiny quivering sensation trembled in her stomach. She wanted to look away, to break the spell that seemed to have bound her in silent stillness.

'Rebecca.'

Only the frantic flutter of eyelashes suddenly oddly heavy and anxious to close over eyes gone slumbrous with emotion and desire betrayed her awareness of the intent beneath the way Frazer said her name.

She knew he was going to kiss her. Knew it and did nothing to escape from it, only trembling violently when his mouth touched hers.

Her hands lifted automatically to clutch him, then dropped as caution sent warning messages to her brain, but Frazer had seen the small movement and his hands came down, hard fingers circling her wrists, slowly stroking the thudding pulse points that pounded so erratically beneath her skin, before lifting her arms and guiding them around his neck. His lips moved on hers and she realised that he was speaking to her.

'Help me, Rebecca,' he demanded. 'If you *really* don't love him any more, if you *really* want to save his marriage, then help me make this look so real that he won't be in any doubt about how much you want me.'

Somewhere in the distance, she could still hear Rory whistling…just. But it wasn't that to which she listened. It was the sound of Frazer's voice, the plea he was making to her. His body was pressing hers down into the mattress. Her fingers were brushing against the thick dark hair that grew into his nape. Beneath her clothes, she could feel the mindless surge of need taking over her body, the aching, tormenting thrill of pleasure that coiled through her at being here with him like this.

She made a soft sound beneath her breath which he obviously mistook for assent, because suddenly he was kissing her, really kissing her as she had once, long ago, dreamed of him doing.

She had no defences against what he was doing to her, either physically or emotionally. It was like falling off the top of a very high cliff, in that once the fall had begun there was no way of stopping it.

Her fingers burrowed into his hair, exploring the hard bones that shaped his head and then dropped to his throat, tracing its curve into his shoulder. Wholly absorbed in the pleasure of touching him, of feeling the hard, hot reality of his flesh, she pushed aside the cotton of his shirt and spread her hand flat against his collarbone, parting her lips to the fierce invasion of his tongue, listening only to what her heart was telling her, and ignoring the frantic warnings of her head.

Her lips clung eagerly to Frazer's, absorbing the fierce pressure of his kiss, her fingers curling into the muscle of his shoulder and feeling it clench, knowing that it was the sensation of her touch that was responsible for his tension.

When she felt his hand on the buttons of her blouse, it was her turn to tense, her fingers locking round his wrist as she tried to tug his hand away, the sounds of protest she was making beneath his mouth inarticulate murmurs, until he lifted his head and breathed softly against her ear, 'It's all right, I'm not going to hurt you. I just want...'

What he just wanted was never said, because he had used his free hand to slip her buttons from their anchoring buttonholes and had exposed the pale delicacy of her body to his gaze. A gaze which he seemed in no hurry to remove from the soft thrust of her breasts, imperfectly concealed by the fragility of her lace bra.

'Frazer!' she protested, but he wasn't listening to her. He was too busy removing her bra.

'Frazer!' she protested more strongly this time, shivering in a mixture of reaction and tension, all too appallingly conscious that if her body kept on reacting to the pleasure of his touch and gaze the way it was doing right now, it wouldn't be much longer before he realised exactly how she felt about him.

In an effort to deflect his attention, she tugged on his wrist, but he ignored her.

An unfamiliar dark surge of colour burned his skin. His eyes, when he slowly focused on her face, glittered with an unfamiliar intensity of emotion.

Rory was forgotten. Everything was forgotten as Frazer shifted his weight slightly against her and then reached out and brushed the erect tip of one breast with the pad of his thumb.

'When I saw you like this, this morning...'

The words were slow and husky, as though they had been dragged from somewhere deep inside him and given voice reluctantly. He moved again, tensing his body, and Rebecca realised shockingly that he was fully aroused.

'Rebecca...' She shuddered as his arms went round her, sliding inside her shirt and across her bare back. 'I want to feel you against me...all of you,' she heard him groan into her ear. 'I want to touch you and taste you.' He shuddered now, much more deeply than she had done, crushing her against his body, so that the roughness of his shirt rubbed against her exposed breasts, the sensation of his body moving erotically against her, stimulating them so that she wanted to claw at his shirt, and remove the barrier that denied her the intimate physical contact her flesh now craved.

'What is it about you, Rebecca, that makes both Rory and me...'

Rebecca froze instantly, desire cooling so rapidly that she shivered in the icy shock of reality.

'Rory,' she managed to whisper unevenly as Frazer raised his head and looked at her, trying to remind him that Rory must have gone, but to her shock his grip on her tightened and he said harshly,

'No, not Rory, damn you! Frazer...I'm *Frazer*, Rebecca!' then as she protested, he too suddenly froze as the meaning of what she had been trying to say sank in.

He released her immediately, turning away from her and sitting on the edge of the bed.

'I'm sorry about that,' he apologised abruptly as she struggled to fasten her blouse, with fingers that suddenly seemed unable to perform this simple task.

Frazer wasn't looking at her, but that didn't make any difference. She was humiliatingly conscious of all that she had come so dangerously close to revealing.

It was different for him; he was a man...a man could betray physical arousal without feeling the slightest degree of emotional involvement.

'I think we'd better go back downstairs,' Rebecca

suggested, ignoring both his apology and the hand he stretched out to help her off the bed, cautiously moving to its other side and standing up there. She had to lean against the mattress to support herself, she felt so weak and shaky.

Frazer turned to look at her, an expression in his eyes she couldn't read, other than that it held a weariness of spirit that made her ache with understanding and compassion.

He was, after all, doing what he thought was right, protecting the twins from their father's weakness, trying to preserve Rory's marriage from that same weakness.

In a totally different way, it must have been as much of a shock to him as it had been to her that he could be aroused physically by her proximity.

'I am sorry,' he reiterated quietly. 'Believe me, I had no intention of...'

'Please!' She had to stop him before he said the words that would destroy her already vulnerable defences. It was one thing to know that she was the last woman on earth he would really want to make love to; it was entirely another to hear him saying so.

'It doesn't matter,' she told him quickly. 'I...I do understand.'

'Do you?' The harsh bitterness of the question shocked her. 'Something else I have my brother to thank for, no doubt. You're right,' he added curtly. 'We'd better get downstairs before they send out a search party. Aunt Maud has old-fashioned ideas about the behaviour of engaged couples.'

Rebecca frowned.

'But you said you were going to tell her that we aren't really engaged.'

'I had second thoughts. I decided it wasn't fair to burden her with the responsibility of keeping the truth from Rory. She's already got enough to cope with. She isn't a young woman, Rebecca,' he reminded her harshly, 'and although she'd kill me for saying so, her memory isn't what it used to be. She could quite easily forget and come out with the truth.'

Rebecca wanted to rail against him for his high-handedness in making his decision without consulting her, but fair-mindedly she had to acknowledge that what he had said about Aunt Maud was quite true.

As he opened the bedroom door for her, she wondered bitterly why it was that he, who was so grimly unforgiving of her, could so compassionately and caringly make allowances for the weaknesses of others. Even Rory.

But then she had already given herself the answer in that one word—caring. Frazer cared for those others: the twins, Maud, Rory... He felt nothing for her. Nothing other than a brief physical desire to which her own body had shamed her in its immediate and overwhelming response.

Halfway down the stairs, she turned to him and said hurriedly, 'This dinner tonight—I don't think...'

'We're going,' Frazer countered arrogantly, then softened that arrogance by adding, 'Gayle Chalmers will have gone to a lot of trouble to entertain us. She's lonely, Rebecca, and very anxious to make friends.'

'But I shan't be staying up here long enough,' Rebecca started to protest, and was silenced by the odd look that flickered in his eyes.

'She doesn't know that,' he told her quietly. 'She believes we're engaged. She'll interpret your refusal of their invitation as a rejection of her personally.'

Rebecca wasn't listening to his explanation. She stared at him and demanded, 'But how does she *know* we're engaged? No one knows, apart from the family here at Aysgarth.'

For a moment Frazer looked almost uncomfortable, his expression reminiscent of that of Helen when she was trying to be particularly devious. Suspicion stirred in Rebecca's brain, but she dismissed it immediately as impossible. Frazer would never have volunteered the information himself.

'Mrs Norton knows…so probably does the doctor,' he pointed out calmly. 'These things have a habit of getting around.'

'But the Institute is twelve miles away from here,' Rebecca protested.

She knew she was worrying at what was really a relatively unimportant issue like a terrier at a rabbit-hole, but so much had been taken out of her control, so much had happened to her recently which left her feeling vulnerable and on edge, that she was almost desperately clinging to something over which she *could* exercise her own strength of will.

'Does it matter *how* she knows?' Frazer asked her sharply, suddenly looking very tired. 'If you won't come with me tonight, I expect I'll manage to find some excuse.' He gave her another brooding look that prickled her nerve-endings, sending a *frisson* of too familiar sensation burning under her skin. It was ridiculous that she should be so vulnerable to him.

Ridiculous and…dangerous.

'Besides, the doctor's due to see you this afternoon, isn't he? He might not consider you fit enough to go out.'

Contradictorily, instead of clinging to this escape, Rebecca heard herself saying crossly, 'Of course he will! There's absolutely nothing wrong with me now, Frazer.'

'No?' he asked her with fine irony, reaching out unexpectedly to cup her face in his palm and turn her into the light so that he could examine her face. 'How long is it since you looked at yourself properly? You're too pale, you've lost weight. And if you're going to tell me that it was the shock of realising you were in my arms and not Rory's that made you tremble as though you were about to pass out on me not fifteen minutes ago, then forget it,' he said flatly. 'We're neither of us unintelligent human beings, Rebecca.'

His hand dropped away from her face, setting her free as he waited for her to precede him down the stairs.

He had a meeting in the afternoon, he explained to Maud, who met them in the hall, but he would be back later in the afternoon.

Rebecca watched him go with a familiar sense of loss. She was too old, surely, to waste her time mooning over a man who would never want her?

'Ah, the devoted fiancée!' taunted Rory, walking into the sitting-room where she was watching Frazer drive away. 'The perfect ending, isn't it? But you aren't married to him yet, Rebecca. My being here is going to remind him of things my lordly, moralistic brother would much rather forget. He'll find the fact that I was your lover first very hard to stomach.'

Rebecca turned on him, frowning. 'You know very well we were never lovers!'

'I know it, and you know it, but Frazer doesn't know it, does he? He won't like knowing that I had you first,' he told her brutally.

'That's not true!'

'Frazer believes it,' he told her softly, watching her frustrated anger with amused enjoyment. 'You obviously haven't been able to convince him otherwise—and of course you can't prove it to him.'

Couldn't she? That was what Rory thought! There was one way she could prove beyond any shadow of a doubt that Rory hadn't been her lover, Rory or indeed any other man, but since Frazer really didn't care how many lovers she had or had not had, the fact that there had been none, that her love for him had kept her from loving any other man enough to share such intimacy with him, was of no interest to him.

'Rory, why are you doing this?' she asked quietly. '*Why* are you trying to destroy our...our engagement? *Why* do you want to hurt me so much?'

'Hurt *you*?' he gave a bitter laugh. 'You, my dear Rebecca, don't come into this other than as something, or rather someone, that my dear brother cherishes. You or any other woman...it's immaterial.

Of course, it helps that it *is* you, since dear old Frazer so obviously and painfully still believes that we were lovers. Odd, that. I never thought that after all these years...' Rory stopped and smiled at her, a smile totally without compunction and kindness. 'Even you, with your naïve outlook on life, must have realised by now that brotherly love is the very last thing I feel for Frazer. Brotherly hate is more like it.'

'But why?' demanded Rebecca.

Rory shrugged. 'Why not?' And then seeing that she was not to be fobbed off he said curtly, 'Why don't you ask my dear brother? God knows, he fought hard enough to stop me from marrying Lillian in the first place.' He gave a harsh laugh. 'Perhaps if he hadn't done so, I wouldn't have married her. But once I was married and ready to acknowledge that I'd made a mistake, would he help me? No. Suddenly dear Frazer turns all moralistic and announces that I should stay married.'

'He worries about the twins,' Rebecca told him. 'But Rory, Frazer can't *force* you to stay married.'

'Can't he? Much you know! Since our parents saw fit to follow tradition and leave everything to Frazer, with me dependent on him for whatever handouts he feels gracious enough to give, the only way I can maintain my current lifestyle and support an ex-wife and those two brats would be if Frazer

put his hand in his pocket and shelled out some of
that money he's so carefully hoarding.'

Rebecca could hardly believe her ears.

'You expect *Frazer* to support your wife and
family?'

Rory glowered at her. 'Why not? He can afford
it. But of course you've got a vested interest in his
finances now, haven't you?'

Rebecca ignored this jibe and said coldly, 'The
only thing that surprises me is that Lillian should
want to stay married to you.'

'She loves me.' Rory said it without compassion
or emotion, and Rebecca suddenly felt desperately
sorry for his wife. She had met Lillian, of course,
but had never really known her.

'But you must feel something for her,' she protested.

He shrugged again.

'She's all right as wives go. She stands to inherit
a nice sum of money from her parents, provided
they don't will it to those two damned brats. Lillian
was OK as a wife, until she got this thing in her
head about the twins needing us here in England.
Still, she's coming to see sense now. While she's
with her parents, she's going to get some info,
about boarding schools.'

'You told Frazer you were thinking of settling

here in England to be near the twins,' Rebecca protested.

'That was Lillian's idea. Besides, do you honestly think he's going to want me here now? A constant reminder that you and I...'

'He'll never let you send the twins to boarding school,' Rebecca told him positively.

Rory laughed.

'He doesn't have much option. After all, they *are* my children.'

'A pity you only seem to remember that fact when you want to use it as a weapon against Frazer,' Rebecca said sharply.

Rory was unconcerned by her contempt.

'Frazer knows what he can do. He can always keep them here with him, after all. How would you like that, Rebecca—starting life with a nice ready-made family, all too ready to show just how much they resent your marrying their precious Uncle Frazer?'

Rory *was* jealous of Frazer, Rebecca recognised sadly. Jealous of him and, because of that jealousy, cruelly determined to do all that he could to hurt him.

'Why?' she whispered more to herself than to Rory, but he heard her and obviously understood, because he stood beside her and gestured through the window.

'Why? God, you really are naïve! Just look around you. Frazer owns all this, Rebecca—and why? Because he's the elder. I hate him for that, and I always have. The more ways I have of hurting him, the happier I'll be. When he got engaged to you, he gave me first prize, didn't he, Rebecca! I'll just bet every time he touches you, every time he makes love with you, he's wondering what it was like for you with me. Oh, he won't say anything, of course—stoical, that's our Frazer—but he'll be thinking it, wondering…and it's going to tear him apart.'

He saw her face and said sourly, 'Pity him, do you?'

'No!' she said, facing him squarely. 'But I do pity you,' and with that she turned and walked out of the room, while her legs would still carry her. Why had she never known, never guessed the hatred Rory felt for Frazer? All those years ago when he had pleaded with her to help him, when he had begged her to save Frazer pain, she had thought how much he loved his brother. She paused, frowning. Rory had had the ideal opportunity to hurt Frazer then, so why hadn't he taken it? Why hadn't he told Frazer the truth about his affair with Michelle? Even if she asked him, she suspected he would not give her a straight answer. She had spoken truthfully when she'd told Rory she pitied him, but she pitied his wife and children even more.

CHAPTER EIGHT

THE doctor, when he arrived, pronounced Rebecca remarkably recovered from her dunking, but warned her that she must still continue to take things easily and that there was still a possibility that the infection could return.

When she asked him tentatively if it was now all right for her to go out, he paused for a moment and then said judiciously, 'Yes, provided you don't overdo things.'

So now she had no excuse for not going to to-night's dinner party. In other circumstances she would have been looking forward to it. After the doctor had gone, she tried not to daydream about how she would have been feeling if she and Frazer *were* really engaged...if he *really* loved her. It was a useless and non-profitable exercise, more worthy of the teenager she had once been, surely, than the woman she now was, but she recognised that what she had learned from Rory had disturbed her, and acknowledged that it was easier to daydream im-possibly romantic dreams of Frazer than to face up to the reality of Rory's envy and resentment of his elder brother.

Comparing it with the loving relationship she shared with Robert, she felt desperately sorry for Frazer, who as far as she could see had always taken a very caring and responsible attitude towards Rory.

From her window, she could see the twins trudging up the drive. It had been a wet, chilly day, not summery at all, and Peter paused to splash enthusiastically in a deep puddle of water, while his sister waited disapprovingly.

Rebecca did not envy their mother, torn as she must be between her love for Rory and her love for her children. And as for the twins themselves... It was no wonder they were so attached to Frazer. She daren't think about the possible consequences for them if Rory had his way and they were sent away to school. They were still too young and far too vulnerable, especially Helen, to be separated from the one person who had given their life its only stability.

She comforted herself with the knowledge that Frazer would not let them go easily, and wondered wryly if part of the purpose of Rory's earlier conversation had been to drive another wedge between Frazer and herself by making it clear to her that the twins were all too likely to remain in Frazer's care.

If she had ever been tempted to take Rory into her confidence and admit to him that her supposed engagement was a 'sham' invented by Frazer to protect *his* marriage, that temptation had gone. She was no threat to Rory's marriage, but if Rory knew the truth he would use it unmercifully against Frazer, and she could not allow that to happen.

She went downstairs to greet the twins as they came into the kitchen, helping them off with their coats and wellingtons, then going out to help Mrs Norton unload the shopping from her small car. She had taken the twins with her into town, as she put it, 'to give Maud and Rebecca a break.'

Over milk and biscuits Rebecca listened to Peter describing the car he had seen in Horthorpe. A strained truce now existed between the twins and herself, one she was careful not to destroy by pushing herself too far into their lives. After all, she would soon be gone, and ultimately it would be someone else's task to reassure them gently that Frazer's marriage would not mean their exclusion from his life.

'Dad says he's going to send us away to school,' Peter announced suddenly, giving her an anxious look.

'Uncle Frazer won't let him,' Helen interrupted quickly, giving Rebecca a look that dared her to deny her statement.

Rebecca said nothing, but she was deeply concerned. She knew now that Rory wouldn't stop to concern himself with his children's feelings in his determination to hurt Frazer.

She wished there was some way she could sit down with Frazer and talk honestly with him, tell him what she had learned, warn him... About what? About Rory's resentment of him? Frazer was an astute, intelligent man. He must already know what his brother felt.

Even so, when she went upstairs to prepare for her evening out she was wearily conscious of the double burden of deceit she now felt she was carrying.

SHE HADN'T BROUGHT any real evening clothes with her, not having anticipated when she'd packed that she would be going out to dinner, but luckily she had put in a black suit which, although far from new, would with a bit of luck carry her through the evening.

It had been a joint Christmas present from Robert, Ailsa and her parents three years ago, outrageously expensive and so simply understated that it was not until it was on that one realised just why its designer was so highly praised. The matt fabric had a slightly ribboned effect that leavened the plainness of the black fabric. The long jacket was cut like a tunic and the short straight skirt, now back in fashion, clung sleekly to her hips and thighs. Having checked that the suit did not need pressing, Rebecca wondered how much longer Frazer was going to be, cravenly almost hoping that he had changed his mind and cancelled the engagement after all.

He walked into the television room while she was sitting with the twins, listening to the news. As usual Helen flew to greet him, and Rebecca had to avert her eyes as he swung the little girl up in his arms and kissed her.

'No Rory?' he asked when he had greeted Peter in much the same way.

'Daddy's gone out,' Helen informed him importantly, then scowled as she added, 'He said he was sick and tired of being here. I don't care. I want him to go away. I don't like it when he's here.'

Over their heads Rebecca saw Frazer's mouth tighten.

'I've told Mrs N. that we won't be in for dinner tonight,' he said to her, and hesitated as though almost waiting for her to argue with him.

Instead she said as calmly as she could, 'The doctor said there was no reason why I shouldn't go out, provided I was sensible.'

Helen, quite obviously not liking being excluded

from their conversation, interrupted eagerly, 'Can we come with you too, Uncle Frazer?'

Rebecca's heart sank as Frazer shook his head and she saw the small face crumple into a sulking scowl.

'It's not fair! We never see you any more now that *she's* here!' Helen protested bitterly.

Rebecca waited for Frazer to placate the little girl, and was surprised when he said firmly, 'That's not true, Helen,' then he softened his statement by adding, 'I thought we'd already talked about how having Rebecca here won't alter how I feel about you.'

'It will when you marry her,' Helen told him bitterly. 'Daddy says you'll send us away then. That she'll make you send us away,' she added with a challenging look at Rebecca.

To her surprise Frazer looked at her and suggested calmly, 'Shall we let Rebecca tell us herself how she feels about having you two living here?'

While she applauded his diplomacy and calm good sense, Rebecca couldn't help feeling trapped and resentful. It wasn't fair of him to push her into making promises to the twins that she wouldn't be here to keep, but they were all three waiting for her to say something.

Remembering all the times she had dealt with the tears and miseries of a small child fighting his or her resentment of the arrival of a new brother or sister, she summoned that experience to her aid and said slowly, 'Love isn't like a piece of cake, Helen. When it has to be shared with more people it doesn't mean that everyone has to have a smaller slice. You know that when two people get married it's because they love one another and because they want to make one another happy. It wouldn't make Frazer very happy if I asked him to send you and Peter away, would it?'

After a brief and rather obvious inward tussle with herself, Helen shook her head.

'Does that mean that because you love Uncle Frazer, you want us to stay?' Peter asked her thoughtfully.

'Yes,' she agreed simply. After all, it was no less than the truth.

'But Daddy said...' Helen began determinedly.

'Daddy made a mistake,' Rebecca interrupted her quietly. 'You see, I love Frazer very much indeed, Helen. I don't want to make him sad, and it would make him very sad indeed if I asked him to send you away.'

'He wouldn't do it anyway,' Peter told her defiantly.

Rebecca laughed and agreed. 'No, I don't think he would!'

Her laughter defused the situation, the tension

going out of both small faces, but for how long? Rebecca wondered as she excused herself, saying that it was time she got ready.

Neither she nor Frazer could give any promises on Rory's intentions. If he decided to send them to boarding school in spite of his brother... She shivered a little and wondered if there was any point in appealing to their mother.

She was now firmly convinced that, whatever he might have told Frazer, Rory had no intention whatsoever of settling down in England and providing a home for his wife and children. If Lillian wanted to keep her husband, she would be obliged to go back to Hong Kong with him, and that would mean leaving the children here at Aysgarth, or sending them away to school.

An hour later, when she rejoined Frazer downstairs, Rebecca was still worrying about the children's future.

Like her, he had changed, and she hesitated on the bottom step of the stairs, caught off guard by her reaction to the sight of him in a dark formally tailored suit and a crisp white shirt, brilliantly light against the darkness of his skin and hair.

He swung round, and frowned when he saw her halting in mid-step, demanding harshly, 'Not going to change your mind, I hope?'

Change your mind? About what? Rebecca felt

dizzy with the shock of the feelings burning her flesh—the compulsion to stretch out and touch him, to smooth her hand over the dark fabric of his suit and feel the hardness of the muscled body it sheathed, to reach up on tiptoe and place her mouth against his, feeling its hardness soften and then harden again in passionate response to her caress.

'Rebecca?' She caught the sharp note of enquiry in his voice just in time and pulled herself together.

'No, I'm not going to change my mind,' she told him, striving to appear calm.

He was looking at her now, and she wondered what he saw. A small, perhaps almost too thin blonde woman, with grey eyes that sometimes looked blue, and a face that must almost be as familiar to him as his own. Certainly there was nothing in the sight of her that could unleash within him the feelings now tormenting her, and the reason for that betraying tightness in his jaw could only be her own tardiness in getting downstairs a few minutes later than she had said.

That had been because she had been unable to resist the impulse to go into the twins' rooms just before she left. Both of them were in bed. Frazer had already been in to read them a story, Helen had announced truculently. The implication was clear enough. They neither wanted nor needed her, and yet as she turned back to the door she had surprised in Helen's eyes a fear that made her hesitate, wanting to reassure her that she was not going to take Frazer away from them, and yet knowing that nothing she could say would carry the kind of conviction that Helen needed.

'I'm sorry I'm late,' she apologised to Frazer. 'I called in on the twins on my way down.'

Now she saw that she *had* surprised him.

'What will you do if Rory insists on sending them away to school?' she asked him as he opened the front door for her.

'What makes you think he might?' he countered. 'Unless of course you've been discussing the subject with him.'

The hostility in his voice made her sigh, wishing there was some way she could push aside the past and talk to him simply as another human being, who was equally concerned about the twins' future.

It was cool outside, a very unsummery breeze blowing off the hills. It raised goosebumps on her skin as she walked over to Frazer's car. She hadn't brought a suitable evening jacket with her; the anorak she *had* brought was hardly suitable for wearing over her elegant designer suit.

She saw Frazer frown as he unlocked the car door, and wondered if he was dreading the evening ahead as much as she was herself. Hardly. What, after all, was there for him to dread, apart from several hours spent in her unwanted company?

'Does your colleague live very far away?' she asked him politely as he started the engine.

'Six miles the other side of the Institute,' he told her. 'They lived in Hampshire before coming up here and, as I said, it's a big adjustment for Gayle to make. She's not much older than you.' He frowned again. 'The work Alan does is very demanding—demanding enough to put a strain on the best of marriages. We're desperately understaffed at the Institute at the moment, and Government cutbacks don't help. Alan told me that Gayle had been complaining about the hours he's been working. Naturally, if it came to a choice, he'd have to put her first. I don't want to lose him.'

'*Naturally?*' Rebecca couldn't resist questioning, her eyebrows lifting. 'There aren't many men these days who *would* put their wife's loneliness before their own career prospects. After all, that hardly goes with the high-powered, geared-for-success image we're all supposed to project these days. He must love her a great deal.'

She wondered if her envy showed in her voice, but she couldn't help imagining what it would be like to be loved like that…and by Frazer.

'He does, but I'm probably being unfair to Gayle. I doubt very much if she'd ask him to choose between her and his job, but she *is* lonely and unsettled.'

'Do they have a family?' asked Rebecca, interested despite herself.

'Not as yet. There was to have been a child, but Gayle had a miscarriage.'

Rebecca made a small sound of sympathy.

'In Hampshire she worked part-time for a friend who owned a dress shop. I suspect she finds time hanging too heavily on her hands up here, although Alan says that there's a lot of work to be done on the house they've bought. I think you'll like her,' Frazer added unexpectedly.

Rebecca's eyebrows rose. 'Does it matter one way or the other? After all, I'm hardly likely to be around for very long.'

'No, you're not, are you?' Frazer agreed evenly, and as she subsided into silence, Rebecca wondered what had prompted her own remark: an idiotic hope that he might stop the car and tell her passionately and unbelievably that she was wrong and that he never intended to let her go? Idiotic indeed. That might be the stuff of romances, but it was not the fabric of real life.

They drove along roads familiar to Rebecca from her childhood, growing up in the area; past the gates to the Institute and through the small pass where the road started to drop down towards the village where Alan Chalmers and his wife lived.

FRAZER HAD BEEN right when he'd predicted that she would like their hostess, Rebecca acknowledged halfway through the evening. The other woman had a vulnerability about her that Rebecca recognised and responded to. Gayle was ruefully honest about her loneliness since coming to Cumbria.

'I expect if I hadn't lost the baby I was expecting, things would have been much better,' she said frankly when she and Rebecca were alone. 'We've been told to wait a few months before trying again.' She pulled a face. 'Nothing should go wrong this time, but I feel guilty because I know how much Alan is worrying about me. This job is a good career move for him, and I'd hate to do anything to prejudice his success in it.' She pulled another face. 'I never dreamed when we first came up here that I was going to feel like this. I even miss my mother,' she added ruefully. 'The village is lovely but lonely.'

Rebecca sympathised with her, and found herself agreeing warmly to Gayle's suggestion that they have lunch together one day, and then wishing she had not been so impetuous. She hated lying like this, deceiving people, letting them believe that she and Frazer were really engaged.

'What's wrong?' Frazer asked her when they were on their way home.

She looked at him in the darkness of the car and frowned.

'Why should anything be wrong?'

'I don't know, but you've been sitting there ever since we left the Chalmers' looking as though you've all the cares in the world on your shoulders.'

'I hate deceiving people,' she told him crossly. 'I hate being in such an invidious position, lying...'

Frazer gave a short bitter laugh.

'That's rich, coming from you! You didn't seem to mind the lies and deceit when you were Rory's lover.'

There was nothing she could say to that, even though she was tempted to fling the truth at him. What good would it do now? And wouldn't he be bound to want to know why she had made such a sacrifice?

They were less than two miles from Aysgarth when he stopped the car, pulling it off the empty road. Rebecca stared at him in perplexity and demanded uncertainly, 'Why have you stopped?'

The look he gave her was derisory and slightly bitter. 'We're supposed to be engaged, remember.'

She still didn't understand. 'So?'

Frazer pulled a handkerchief out of his pocket and handed it to her.

'So I think it would be a good idea if you wiped off your lipstick. Rory won't be in bed yet, even if Maud is.'

As the significance of what he was saying struck her, she went red and then white, pushing the handkerchief back at him and saying fiercely, 'We're not teenagers, Frazer, and surely long past the age of making love in cars. And even if you had supposedly stopped the car to…to kiss me, it would be perfectly natural for me to have re-applied my lipstick. Besides,' she added almost pleadingly, 'it will stain your handkerchief and the stain probably won't come out.'

'Re-applied your lipstick?' He turned in his seat to look at her, a hard, disturbing look that made her pulses race frantically. '*That* hardly suggests a passionate relationship, does it?'

Her heart was beginning to thud hurriedly.

'You want Rory to believe that…'

'I want Rory to know the moment he sets eyes on you that there's only one thing on both our minds, and that one thing is how quickly we can be alone to resume the lovemaking our very deep and passionate love for one another has made us unable to control. I want him to look at you and know that you'll be spending the night in my bed, in my arms—and that it won't be for the first time.'

Her small gasp of shock made him smile coldly at her.

'You think it impossible for us to be so convincing? Have you forgotten, then, so quickly, that no matter what you and I might feel about one another as human beings, on a physical level the sexual chemistry between us—'

'No!' Rebecca denied sharply, not letting him finish. Her face and body felt hot with chagrin and dread. She ought to have known that he would have recognised her responsiveness to him, and, even if he could casually dismiss his own sexual arousal, knowing the truth she could not listen with equanimity to what he was saying.

'No?' Frazer turned the word into a soft threat that made her nerve-endings jangle. 'Are you asking for proof?'

Proof? *Proof* was the last thing she wanted. Rebecca turned her head to tell him so and found herself mesmerised by the heart-shaking proximity of his body.

'Besides,' he told her dulcetly, 'this will probably be far more effective, and it *will* save my handkerchief.'

She tried to move away and found she couldn't…couldn't do anything other than sit there almost stupefied as he lowered his head and brushed his mouth slowly across her own.

It wasn't what she had been expecting; it wasn't the brief businesslike press of his mouth against her own, a disciplined, controlled exercise designed to underline his superiority; and, because it wasn't what she had been expecting, she had no defences against it.

Frazer's mouth brushed hers as softly as silk, feathering slowly against her lips, lingering. He moved in his seat, his hands on her waist, and she prayed that he would not recognise the long tremor that shook her body for what it was. He made a sound in his throat, something that her senses recognised and responded to, and as though she had given him some hidden signal she herself didn't recognise he crushed her back against her seat and kissed her as, she recognised distantly, she had been aching for him to do for far too long.

There was no way she could resist it, no way either that she could disguise her response to him. Even without touching him, even without doing anything, she was already betraying her response to him. Beneath her thin suit-jacket her nipples peaked and ached. There was nothing she wanted more than the touch of his hands on her skin, his lips...

She shuddered and made a soft sound of anguish in her throat as he bit at her mouth, her body arching up to his, everything forgotten in the need that he had unleashed inside her. The sensation of his hands caressing her body, moulding it through the layers of her suit and underwear, maddened her with its tormenting promise of what it would be like to have those hands against her skin with nothing between them.

Quite when she reached out and slid her hands under his jacket, smoothing her palms feverishly first against his shirt, and then against the moist heat of his bared chest, she had no idea; she knew only that the sensation of rough hair and satiny skin caused the twisting ache tormenting her lower stomach to intensify to such a pitch that she actually moaned a husky protest when Frazer lifted his mouth from hers to look down at where her hands lay against his body.

'I could take you now and make you forget that Rory ever existed,' he told her rawly.

Sickly Rebecca withdrew from him as though he had struck her, her eyes glazing with tears of shock and bewilderment. She couldn't bear to look at the shadowy darkness of his exposed chest. She had no memory of wrenching those buttons from their fastening, no memory of pulling off his tie—and yet she must have done so.

Although he refastened all but the top button of his shirt, he didn't replace his tie. He had got what he wanted, she thought despairingly, as he set the car in motion once more. There was no need for him to look so grim and bitter.

She was tempted to replace her lipstick, but one sickening glance at her mouth in the mirror had shown her that no amount of lipstick was going to disguise its swollen fullness, and that anyone looking at her was going to know exactly how she had come by those two tiny betraying marks that showed where Frazer's teeth had raked her mouth's softness. She burned with misery and humiliation as she remembered how she had responded to that small violence, how she had almost encouraged him to repeat the fierce caress.

'We're home.' The curtness of Frazer's voice brought her back to reality, and she flushed again as she realised that the car was motionless.

Once out of the car she hurried on ahead of Frazer, desperate to escape to the privacy of her room. The hallway was brilliantly illuminated, and she stopped, dazzled for a moment, and unwittingly giving Frazer the opportunity to catch up with her and to slide a possessive arm around her waist, as the sitting-room door opened and as though on cue Rory walked out. Only he wasn't alone. Lillian was with him, a Lillian who looked both tired and angry.

The look she gave Rebecca tightened her mouth

for a moment, then she said coolly, 'Rory tells me congratulations are in order. A pity we'll probably be back in Hong Kong before you get married.'

'Back?' Frazer turned to Rory and said grimly, 'I thought you'd decided to become UK-based.'

Rory shrugged dismissively, and Lillian gave him an anxious look as she caught the repressive tone of Frazer's voice.

'We did think about it,' she said quickly, 'but…'

'But since I don't have your financial advantage, my dear brother, I can't afford to whistle several thousand pounds a year down the wind, which I would be doing if we moved back to the UK. However, we do have *some* good news for you, don't we, my love?' he said smoothly. 'Lillian has made us an appointment for tomorrow to go and look at a boarding school that's been recommended to her. It's in the south of England…'

It was Rebecca who interrupted him, too angry to check the impulsive words of protest that rose to her lips. 'But surely the twins would be better off here?' she said fiercely.

Lillian seemed about to say something, but Rory silenced her, saying softly, 'Oh, we couldn't be so selfish. Once you and Frazer are married, you won't want those two brats hanging around, and so I've told them,' he added carelessly, disregarding both his wife's anguished look and Frazer's frown. 'Of course you're welcome to join us tomorrow when we go to look at the school. With your expertise, Rebecca, you'll be able to give us your professional opinion.'

Carried away on a wave of rage against Rory and compassion for Frazer and the twins, Rebecca said sharply, 'Of course we'll go with you. Frazer will want...'

She broke off, suddenly aware of how much she was taking for granted, and was relieved to hear Frazer saying coldly, 'Rebecca is quite correct. I just wish you'd consulted me first. There are plenty of excellent schools locally, where the children would at least be able to come home for the weekend.'

'Nothing's been firmly decided as yet,' Rory told them carelessly. Some private pleasure was making his eyes glitter with amused malice, and the look he was giving them both made Rebecca's heart thump uncomfortably. 'It will mean an overnight stay, you realise?' and when Frazer gave him a curt nod of assent, he added equally casually, 'Right, then. Lillian will sort out the hotel booking. Someone's recommended a decent hotel reasonably close to the school.'

And even then Rebecca didn't realise the danger both she and Frazer were stepping into.

CHAPTER NINE

THEY set out early, all of them travelling in Frazer's car, after an uncomfortable breakfast with the twins, neither of whom addressed more than a single word to their parents.

Rebecca felt heart-stoppingly sorry for Lillian, who was plainly unhappy with the situation, and who was very obviously torn between her love for Rory and her love for the twins.

Rebecca wondered sadly if there would ever come a day when she might regret having put Rory first, and suspected that there very likely would. He was a selfish, spoilt man, incapable of loving anyone other than himself. Several times during the long drive, he deliberately tried to needle Frazer, and Rebecca could only marvel at the latter's calm, unruffled ability to turn Rory's jibes harmlessly aside.

The name of the boarding school recommended to Lillian was only vaguely familiar to Rebecca. She was sitting in the front passenger seat next to Frazer, and she wondered if he was feeling as tense as she was herself. He must be concerned about the twins and their future, but he hid his anxiety well. In fact of all of them, the only one who was displaying any visible emotion was Rory, who was almost lit up with a mixture of anticipation and triumph that made her own nervousness increase.

It was a long, tiring journey, not made any easier by the heavy holiday traffic and the long motorway delays for roadworks.

Rebecca wondered whether it was because she was still not back to one hundred per cent fitness that she felt so on edge and exhausted, and if she was the only one to be so keenly conscious of the tension within the luxurious car.

Rory had already made one jibe at the difference between his own situation and Frazer's. He had to drive a cheap rented car, while Frazer owned a new registration Daimler saloon.

If she hadn't known from a remark of her own mother's that Frazer had given Rory a very large sum of money indeed on his twenty-fifth birthday, equal to virtually half the value of the estate, because he had felt that the law of primogeniture was unfair, it would have been all too easy, listening to Rory's conversation, to believe that Frazer had virtually cheated him out of his inheritance.

More than once Rebecca found herself having to

clench her jaw to stop herself from flying to Frazer's defence.

She could well understand why Frazer said nothing, did nothing that might antagonise Rory. Not with the twins' future at stake.

She wished she knew Lillian well enough to take her on one side and plead with her to at least allow the twins to remain with Frazer, if she and Rory weren't prepared to either have them with them in Hong Kong or to settle permanently in the UK. A boarding school existence without the leavening of love both she and Robert had received from their parents, without the frequent visits and holidays with them, that she suspected the twins would not have, would leave emotional scars which she felt would never heal.

But Lillian, obviously believing that she and Rory had once been lovers, was openly antagonistic towards her, addressing what conversation she did make to her husband and Frazer and virtually totally excluding Rebecca.

They stopped for lunch once they were south of London and free of its traffic. Even though Frazer did not allow them to linger over the meal, it was gone two-thirty when they eventually set off. Their appointment was at four, and, while Rory congratulated himself on picking a school which was going to be within relatively easy driving distance of the city and the airport, Frazer's mouth tightened in anger.

Was he thinking as she was, Rebecca wondered, that it would be impossible for him to drive down and see the twins and return in one day, and that that must make it more difficult for him to see them as frequently as he otherwise might?

She came out of her private thoughts to hear Lillian saying, 'You've been so good to the twins, Frazer, but now that you and Rebecca are getting married I agree with Rory that it's probably only fair that you should be allowed to get on with your lives without them.'

Rebecca ached to say that their marriage made no difference, and that the twins should stay at Aysgarth, but almost as though he knew what she was thinking Frazer shot her a darkly warning look that silenced her.

The school had originally been a small Queen Anne manor house. Evidence of its success and prosperity could be seen in the discreet modern additions to the original building. The prospectus which Rebecca had already read offered facilities that made the place sound more like an up-market luxury hotel than a place of education, but it was unfair of her to dismiss the skills of its staff simply because its prospectus seemed to concentrate far more on leisure activities than education ones, she acknowledged.

Out of good manners, and because, after all, the twins were not her children, Rebecca hung back at the rear, when the four of them were shown into the headmaster's study, but to her consternation Rory turned back towards her, and with a malicious smile took her arm, propelling her forward before she could object and exclaiming loudly, 'This is where we're going to need you, Rebecca my lovely, as the expert, so to speak,' and, to complete her embarrassment, as the headmaster rose to greet them Rory introduced her, saying, 'My brother's fiancée...a fellow teacher, who's going to tell us whether or not your school is suitable for the twins.'

Mortification caused a hot flood of colour to burn up under Rebecca's skin as she withstood the headmaster's coolly appraising look. Rory was deliberately humiliating her, but she could see from both Lillian and Frazer's faces that they seemed to think that Rory's behaviour was something the two of them had deliberately planned.

As the headmaster quite deliberately solicitously seated Lillian immediately in front of his desk with Rory at her side, banishing Frazer and of course herself to a very secondary position, Frazer took advantage of her proximity to whisper curtly, 'If I'd genuinely ever entertained any idea of marrying you, your cold-hearted attitude towards the twins' future would have given me very strong second thoughts indeed.'

Her cold-hearted attitude! Rebecca gasped audibly and turned a vivid and angry face towards him.

'It wasn't my idea to send them to boarding school!'

'Maybe not, but you seemed keen enough to suggest coming down here with Rory and Lillian last night. What's the idea, Rebecca? Still hoping for the impossible—that Rory's going to turn his back on his wife and family?'

The headmaster had already begun to speak. He had a sonorous, mellifluent voice which he used to good effect, Rebecca recognised. He was also distancing himself from them to such good effect that she could not make up her mind what she felt about him. He was highly qualified, the school was well subscribed to, and she suspected probably very fashionable, but whether it was the right place for the twins...

She thought of the old-fashioned boarding school she and Robert had attended, less than twenty miles from Aysgarth—a school where the staff had decades of understanding the problems that children faced. A school close enough to Aysgarth for two lonely and unhappy children to feel that they had at least retained some contact with something familiar.

When they eventually left the school all of them were silent, apart from Rory, who commented blithely, 'Well, I don't know about the rest of you, but I'm looking forward to a decent dinner and bottle of decent wine. How far is it to this hotel you've booked us into?' he asked his wife as they waited for Frazer to unlock the door.

'Not far. It's just outside the next village, apparently. A lot of the parents use it when they come to visit their children.' Lillian's face clouded and she said uncertainly, 'Rory, I'm not sure we're doing the right thing. It's so far away from Aysgarth, the children are going to miss it dreadfully—and Frazer.'

'I've told you already, my love, we can't expect Frazer to play daddy to our two brats, not when he's all too likely to have some of his own before too long,' Rory told her.

He didn't look very pleased that she had voiced her doubts, and Rebecca felt her heart lift a little bit. If Lillian could be convinced that the twins would be better off with Frazer...

Before she could change her mind, she said quickly, 'Well, I for one would be quite happy for the twins to stay at Aysgarth.'

She saw that the three of them had focused on

her, Rory frowning his irritation, Lillian looking surprised, and Frazer... What was he thinking behind that grimly cold look he was giving her?

'As an ex-boarding school pupil myself, I know how important it is to feel that you're not completely isolated from your family. We were lucky,' she added diplomatically, 'my parents were able to come home at frequent intervals,' and then, praying that she wasn't doing the wrong thing, she added, 'I know I speak for both Frazer and myself when I say we'd love to have the twins staying with us.' With a mental apology for the lie, she added as convincingly as she could, 'They adore Frazer, and I've become so fond of them myself. Of course,' she went on, all too uncomfortably conscious of the attention now riveted on her, 'we appreciate that the twins' education must be one of your first concerns, but there are several very good schools close to Aysgarth.'

Lillian was looking both relieved and surprised.

'I must admit it would be the ideal solution if the twins *could* continue to stay at Aysgarth.' She turned to Rory. 'I know you feel the same way, darling.' She gave Rebecca a tentative smile. 'Rory was saying only last night that he'd prefer to leave the twins with Frazer, but that he felt it wasn't fair to you to do so.'

Rebecca looked across at Rory just in time to see

the look of irritated chagrin cross his face. So *she* was to have been the scapegoat for his spiteful decision to remove the twins from Frazer's care, was she?

'Not at all,' she quickly reassured Lillian. 'In fact, we'd love to have them living with us, wouldn't we, darling?' she appealed to Frazer, and then, with great daring, walked over to him and slid her arm through his, pressing up against him in what she hoped was a suitably adoring newly affianced manner.

The moment her body touched his, she was aware of his tension. Did he dislike her so much that even such a brief physical contact with her displeased him? And yet it wasn't so long ago that physical contact with her had been responsible for...but no, she mustn't think about that. She must concentrate on doing all she could to stop Rory from ruining the twins' lives. What kind of father was he? she wondered angrily...but then she already knew. Frazer had been right when he'd said that the twins should never have been conceived.

'If it wasn't for this promotion Rory's been offered, we'd probably have made the decision to come home,' Lillian was saying almost apologetically. 'But it's too good a chance to pass over, and Rory is going to need me with him. The promotion involves a good deal of entertaining and socialising.

It would be marvellous if the twins could remain at Aysgarth. If you're sure you won't mind?'

'We won't mind at all,' Rebecca reassured her.

She could almost feel the waves of anger emanating from Rory, and she could see from his face how much he hated being out-manoeuvred, but there was nothing he could do, without admitting to Lillian that the only reason he wanted to send the twins away to school was to get at Frazer.

Now with Lillian turning to him and saying mistily, 'Darling, isn't this wonderful? I'm so relieved! I was dreading telling the twins that they'd have to leave Aysgarth.' She turned to Frazer and Rebecca. 'We're so grateful to you. This new post is only for three years, and with any luck then Rory will be sent back to the UK.'

She might hope for that, but Rebecca doubted that Rory did.

She felt drained, exhausted by the effort of out-manoeuvring Rory. Her legs had turned to jelly, and there was nothing she wanted more than to be able to turn to Frazer and to feel the hard warmth of his body supporting and enveloping her.

Instead she said brightly, 'So that's all settled, then. The twins will stay with us.'

'You can't know what a relief it is to know that they'll be staying on at Aysgarth,' Lillian told her almost chattily as they got into the car. 'I've felt so guilty about the way we're imposing on Frazer, but it's impossible to have them with us in Hong Kong.'

She leaned across Rebecca to give Frazer directions for the hotel.

'It's only quite small,' she told them as they pulled off the road and into a well-kept gravel drive. 'Ten bedrooms, that's all, but the chef-cum-owner was trained by the Roux brothers and the restaurant is virtually booked solid every night.'

The hotel was lovely, but Rebecca was in no mood to appreciate its beauty fully. A tension headache pounded in her temples, and as they stepped forward to the reception desk she was disconcerted to hear the receptionist saying to Rory, 'Ah yes Mr Aysgarth—two double rooms, wasn't it? You were very lucky, sir. Our last two rooms. We've got a party of Japanese visitors booked into all the other rooms.'

Rebecca turned instinctively towards Frazer, her pale face betraying her consternation.

At her side Lillian was saying casually, 'Rory told me that you'd specifically said that you and Frazer wanted to share. I suppose it's very difficult for you—Maud is so old-fashioned.' She pulled a wry face, and Rebecca raised her head to find she was staring blindly into Rory's amused and triumphant eyes.

She tried to speak, to say something, anything, but it was too late. Frazer had signed in for both of them, and a porter was wheeling away their luggage.

'Why don't we all meet down here in the bar in, say, an hour?' Rory was suggesting smoothly, looking at his watch, then he looked at her and added suggestively, 'But maybe the two of you would prefer rather longer?'

REBECCA WAS SHAKING with a mixture of anger and shock as she followed a grimly silent Frazer to the room they had been allocated.

As he unlocked the door, she saw that it was really a very pleasant room; attractively furnished and a good size, but the double bed... She could barely draw her attention away from the double bed, and her anger and shock had coalesced into a sensation of miserable humiliation.

It was only after the porter had brought their overnight cases that Frazer spoke to her, his face hard with temper, his voice savagely icy.

'I didn't want to embarrass you downstairs by demanding an explanation of why you saw fit to tell Rory we wanted a double room. I suppose you were motivated by some idiotic desire to make him jealous. And to think that for a moment this afternoon, I actually believed...'

'*I didn't* ask him to book us this room,' Rebecca interrupted him huskily, but she could see that Frazer didn't believe her. Despair swept over her as she met the coldness in his eyes.

'Oh, can't you see?' she protested. 'He must have guessed that this engagement of ours is just a charade. That's why he did this. He must know that...'

'That what? That you love *him?*'

'I *don't* love him,' Rebecca told him jerkily. She felt sick and very weak. A familiar tightness gripped her chest. She started to cough, fighting to draw breath, and saw Frazer frown.

'Well, it's too late to do anything about it now. You heard what the receptionist said—they're fully booked.'

He looked curtly at the double bed, waiting for her to get her breath back.

'You said you think Rory knows the truth. How *could* he know, unless you've told him?'

Rebecca felt too miserable to argue.

'I'll get changed in the bathroom and then go downstairs and wait for you,' Frazer told her curtly. His frown deepened. 'I haven't thanked you yet for what you said this afternoon.'

She looked uncertainly at him.

'The twins,' he explained grimly. 'Without your timely intervention I suspect Rory would have had them installed in that damned school.'

'He hates you,' Rebecca told him bleakly, and was surprised to receive a startled look of surprise in response followed by an equally surprising, 'Yes, I know. And that's my fault. I should have realised far sooner than I did how much he resented the fact that I inherited Aysgarth. Not because he wants the estate…' His mouth compressed and Rebecca saw that he felt he had already said too much. 'Naturally the fact that I'm supposedly engaged to you doesn't help to endear me to him,' he added.

Rebecca wanted to tell him that he was wrong, that Rory felt nothing for her and never had done, but the moment was gone. Frazer was already picking up his case and heading for the small bathroom. In less than half an hour he emerged dressed in a formal dark suit, his white shirt-front broken by a deep maroon silk tie.

She loved him so much, she acknowledged achingly, as he told her he would wait for her downstairs. If only things were different!

Different! She suppressed a small, bitter laugh. What she needed was a miracle!

When Frazer had gone, she removed the clothes she had travelled in, had a brief shower, then, wrapped in the towelling robe provided by the hotel, sat down to renew her make-up.

When the bedroom door opened, she was surprised, but not alarmed. She had, after all, nothing to fear from Frazer.

Only it wasn't Frazer who had walked into their room; it was Rory.

Rebecca stared at him in concerned surprise, then said uncertainly, 'Rory, what are you doing here?'

He ignored her question and said silkily, 'Aren't you going to thank me, Becca? After all, I've made it possible for you and Frazer to spend the night together. You always did dote on him, didn't you?' He gave her a cynical smile. 'Rushing to throw yourself so nobly into the breach!'

He had brought a glass of whisky with him and now he took a deep swallow from it, draining it.

A frisson of alarm shivered through Rebecca when he walked over to the dressing-table and stood beside her, putting the glass down and studying their reflections in the mirror. When his hand came out and his finger traced the deep V of her robe, she froze.

'I wonder what my dear brother would say if he came in here and saw us together like this now? Do you suppose he would stay engaged to you, Becca, if he thought that you and I had arranged this night away so that we could be together?'

Her whole body had gone numb, only her mind remaining alert and sharp.

Rory had come up here deliberately, had *planned*

that somehow or other Frazer would find them together! Hysteria bubbled up inside her. If only he knew it, his scheming was all so unnecessary. Frazer *didn't* love her, and the anger he would feel on finding them together would be because of the threat that she posed to Rory's marriage, not because he was jealous, but she couldn't tell Rory that.

Rory was standing behind her now, his hands on her shoulders in a pose of pseudo-loverlike adoration.

'Clever of me, wasn't it?' he murmured, bending as though to kiss her neck. 'Arranging all this.'

Rebecca tried to pull away and found to her terror that she was anchored to her chair by the hard grip of his hands; hands that were already beginning to hurt her.

'Rory, don't be ridiculous,' she protested, trying to appear calm and unconcerned. 'I doubt that Frazer *will* come up here. I arranged to meet him in the bar—and besides,' she added with apparent carelessness, suddenly receiving inspiration, 'he knows the truth. I've told him everything.'

'And he believed you?' Rory mocked her, his face suddenly ugly. 'Nice try, my dear, but it won't work—I know my brother too well. Oh, no, it doesn't matter what you say to him now, he'll remain convinced to the day he dies that I was your first lover, even though you and I both know it isn't true.' He gave a self-satisfied laugh. 'How easily you let me manipulate you! You were almost desperate to let me make use of you.'

'I did it for Frazer,' Rebecca told him rawly, her throat dry and sore. 'You *know* that. I did it to stop him finding out that you were having an affair with Michelle.'

'I know that, and you know it, my sweet,' Rory agreed, 'but Frazer will *never* believe it. The pure virginal child-woman he'd posted keep-off fences around for himself, giving herself to me!' Rory shook with laughter. 'And *you* let me do it! *You* let me lie to him and tell him that you were my lover!'

'Because I didn't want him to be hurt by the truth,' Rebecca told him wildly. 'You asked me to help you. You said you were sorry about what had happened...that you wanted to keep the truth from him because he loved Michelle.'

'And so you stepped nobly into her place. Why, I wonder?'

Rebecca gave him a scornful glance through the mirror.

'You know why,' she said coolly. 'I love him.'

'Ah, yes, so you did—all that repressed, intense teenage passion that you were so careful to hide from him. But now you don't have to hide it from him any more, do you, my lovely? What a pity the happy ending is going to be spoiled—and it will be spoiled, Rebecca. He won't marry you now.'

She had been lulled into a state of false security by his casualness, so that when he bent quickly, tugging her to her feet and dragging her into his arms, her frantic struggles were not enough to free herself from the imprisoning grip of his hands. She felt his breath graze her ear and heard him saying triumphantly, 'Aha...right on cue!' as Frazer walked in through the half-open bedroom door, his face grimly set.

Rory was a consummate actor, Rebecca acknowledged sickly, watching as her captor managed to look both guilty and defiant.

She couldn't think of a word to say, she was all too miserably conscious of how they must look to Frazer, but to her astonishment, instead of berating her, Frazer looked only at Rory and ordered icily, 'Let her go this instant, Rory.'

He made no threats, said nothing violent, and yet as he looked at him Rory went pale, stepping back from her almost nervously.

'It was her idea, Frazer,' he said quickly. 'She planned it all. She was the one...'

'Get out,' Frazer interrupted him softly. 'Just get out.'

Alone in the now silent room with Frazer, Rebecca waited for him to speak.

When he did, what he said was so mundane that
it should have released her tension.

'Are your clothes still in the bathroom?' he asked
her, and when she nodded, he told her calmly, 'Perhaps you'd better go and get dressed, then.'

Mutely she did so. When she emerged from the
bathroom, Frazer was just replacing the telephone
receiver.

'I've cancelled our booking,' he told her quietly.
'Can you manage to pack yourself or shall I?'

Could she manage? She gave him a brief look,
wondering if she was merely too shocked to hear
the cynicism in his voice, if she was imagining the
way he was looking at her with something ap-
proaching grave concern, and she shook her head,
too confused by everything that was happening to
find the energy to ask any questions.

'I can manage,' she told him.

Half an hour later they were both in Frazer's car,
heading north. Rebecca was exhausted and yet at
the same time too keyed up to sleep.

She had no idea if he had told Rory and Lillian
that they were leaving, no idea *why* he had not yet
mentioned finding Rory with her. She was too
heartsick to raise the subject herself. She knew
quite well what conclusions he must have drawn
from the scene he walked into. And what did it
matter? Knowing the truth, knowing that there had

never been any relationship with anyone, never mind Rory, wasn't going to alter the way Frazer felt about her...or rather didn't feel.

She closed her eyes and leaned back in her seat, giving a small exhausted sigh that drew Frazer's attention to her face, his mouth setting grimly, and at some point, although she herself had not expected it, she must have fallen asleep, because the next thing she knew was that she was being woken up by Frazer and that it was dark outside.

'Oh, are we home?' she asked in sleepy surprise.

'No, not yet,' he told her. 'I've booked us into a small hotel the receptionist recommended to me. It's in the same group, although apparently not as luxurious. I didn't think either of us was in any condition for the long drive to Cumbria.'

Tiredly Rebecca let him help her out of the car. She swayed slightly on her feet, her body numb with exhaustion, then tensed as she felt the warm bulk of his body supporting her.

The hotel was small and comfortable. The receptionist produced a key, and offered to have a meal served to them in their room since the dining-room had closed.

Frazer looked enquiringly at Rebecca, but she shook her head. Food was the last thing she felt like. She heard Frazer saying something about sandwiches, and then she was being propelled firmly down a corridor and up a flight of stairs.

She was not quite sure why Frazer kept his arm around her as he unlocked the door, unless it was to prevent her from escaping.

Why had he brought her here? she wondered feverishly, as he ushered her inside. So that he could tell her what he thought of her somewhere where there would be no one familiar for her to turn to? So that he...but the look in his eyes as he closed the door and turned to study her was anything but threatening.

'Just tell me one thing,' he said quietly, watching her. 'Is it true that you love me?'

Rebecca swallowed and then gulped, frantically trying to summon up a denial, but her expression had already given her away, and besides, Frazer was far too astute for her to deceive in her present vulnerable state, so she lifted her head proudly and said unsteadily, 'Yes.'

'Oh, Rebecca, *you wretch*!' The words were something between a groan and a protest, and as she blinked at the intensity of them, Frazer came over to her and pulled her into his arms. She was too exhausted to resist.

Against her ear, he demanded thickly, '*Why? Why* did you let me think you loved Rory?'

'I didn't,' she protested. 'I told you I didn't.'

'But you let me go on thinking that you and he had been lovers. You didn't tell me...' He felt the restless movement she made in his arms and tilted her face up to his so that she couldn't avoid looking at him. 'If I hadn't eavesdropped on your argument with Rory this evening, you'd *never* have told me, would you?'

'I didn't think you'd believe me,' she protested, dizzy with confusion and bewilderment.

'Liar,' he said softly. 'You didn't tell me because you knew once you had I'd want to know what prompted you to make that kind of sacrifice. They say listeners never hear any good of themselves. Well, that was true for me tonight. I stood outside that door and learned how much I'd maligned you and misjudged you. And then I heard you saying that you love me,' he ended huskily.

Suddenly Rebecca's self-control snapped and she heard herself saying in a high-pitched, unfamiliar voice, '*Why* have you brought me here? *Why* are you doing this?' and to her consternation her eyes filled with hot tears that spilled on to her skin.

'Rebecca! Rebecca, you little idiot. Hasn't it dawned on you yet that I'm ''doing all this'', as you call it, because I'm crazily in love with you? That I loved you eight years ago and that I've never stopped loving you? That was why I was so savage with you then. *That's* why Rory has been so determined to break us up. You see, Rory knows how I feel about you. He's always known.'

Her tears had stopped. She stared at him in disbelief.

'You love me? But Rory said...'

'Rory lied,' Frazer told her firmly. 'Eight years ago I thought you were too young to be burdened with an adult man's love, but I promise you Rory knew exactly how I felt about you. He lied to both of us, Becca. He let me believe you'd had an affair with him, knowing what it would do to me, and he let you believe I loved someone else.'

Rebecca gave a tight shudder.

'It all seems so unreal. This morning we were enemies. You hated me, and now...'

'No, I never hated you, and we certainly weren't enemies,' Frazer told her softly. 'Why do you think I pushed you into this fake engagement? Why do you think I made sure that as many people as possible knew about it? Think, Rebecca,' he told her, shaking her gently. 'I was hoping that somehow or other I'd be able to make you see that I could give you something Rory couldn't.'

'But all these years! You've kept me away from Aysgarth...'

'Not because I didn't want you there. I wanted it all too badly. I was too proud, too easily convinced

by Rory that you preferred him to me. I told myself
I wasn't prepared to come second to my brother in
your life, and then I saw you again and I knew it
didn't matter a damn what place I had in your life
as long as I could persuade you to share it with me.
Is it true, Rebecca? *Do* you love me?' he asked her,
framing her face in his hands.

'Yes.' The admission trembled past her lips. She
turned her head and said uncertainly, 'You've
booked us a double room.'

Frazer laughed, and she realised with a small
pang how long it was since she had heard him laugh
like that, naturally and easily. Suddenly he looked
younger, gentler.

'As a matter of fact, I've booked two double
rooms, but I suppose I *could* always be persuaded
to share yours, if that's what you want.'

Her heart had started to pound far too heavily.

'Why did you leave the other hotel?' she asked
obliquely.

'Because if we'd stayed, I was afraid I might do
something I've promised myself I'll never do, and
that's use violence against another human being.'
Frazer saw her face and reassured her, 'Not you,
you idiot...never you. I meant Rory. When I stood
in that doorway and saw the look of fear in your
eyes, I could have killed him there and then. I
wanted to kill him,' he added painfully, 'and then

I heard what you were saying to him, and suddenly it wasn't just Rory I hated, it was myself as well...for what I'd done to you in believing him, for what I'd done to *us*.'

He started to kiss her and she trembled wildly in his arms, not the adult woman she was, but suddenly the young girl she had been, desperately and despairingly in love with a man who seemed way, way beyond her.

'You can't know how often I've dreamed of holding you like this,' Frazer whispered fiercely against her mouth, nibbling gently at it, teasing her lips with the tip of his tongue until she was in danger of forgetting everything other than her need to be part of him. 'You were sixteen when I first looked at you and knew that it wasn't merely affection that I felt for you, but you were so young...too young to make the kind of commitment I wanted you to make.' His fingers gently traced the line of her jaw. 'You don't look much older now. Did you know that Rory taunted me with the fact that you'd been lovers, told me how you'd responded to him? How you'd begged him, how you'd said...'

Rebecca silenced him by putting her fingers against his mouth.

'None of it was true,' she told him shakily. 'None of it.'

'No.' Frazer's eyes went bleak. 'I ought to have known, to have guessed. My only excuse is that my love blinded me to the truth.'

Someone knocked on the door and he released her reluctantly. It was the waiter with their sandwiches.

'The very last thing I feel like doing right now is eating,' Frazer whispered as he took Rebecca back in his arms after the waiter had gone. 'I want to stay with you tonight, Rebecca, but the decision must be yours.'

She was a woman now, not a girl, but she still felt oddly shy as she told him, 'I want you to stay, but there's something I should tell you first. I'm not...I don't have any form of...of protection.' She found she couldn't look straight at him. 'You see, I haven't...that is, this...'

'I'm going to be your first lover, and, not having anticipated such a momentous event, you haven't had the forethought to provide yourself with any kind of contraception—is that what you're trying to tell me?'

It was several seconds before she realised that he was quite deliberately teasing her.

'You *knew* all the time!' she protested. 'And you let me...'

'I overheard you telling Rory that there hadn't been anyone,' he admitted, 'but, chauvinist male

that I am, some insecure vulnerable part of me
wanted to hear you saying it.' He was smiling at
her, but there was regret in his eyes. 'I wanted to
hear not just that you loved me but that you trusted
me as well. However, I'm afraid I've spent far too
many nights on my own cursing fate for giving you
to Rory and not to me to be able to place any re-
liance on my own self-control.'

He was already releasing her, moving away from
her, and suddenly Rebecca couldn't bear it.

'Frazer, please don't go,' she begged him.
'Please, I want you to stay.'

She saw him hesitate and her heart trembled.

'If I touch you now, you know what's going to
happen, don't you?' His voice was muffled and
strained, an unfamiliar possessiveness glittering in
his eyes. 'But you'll want to wait until your parents
come home to get married.'

He almost groaned the words, and suddenly her
body was on fire. She took a step forward and said
simply, 'I don't want to wait for anything. We've
already waited far too long.'

'And if I make you pregnant?' Frazer's voice was
strained and harsh.

Rebecca looked him straight in the eye.

'Then we'll tell my parents the truth and explain
to them why we got married without them, very

quickly and very quietly. Besides, it might be for the best. A big wedding could be awkward.'

'Because of Rory?' Frazer asked broodingly. 'He's got one hell of a lot to answer for.'

'Forget him,' Rebecca advised him. And then, with a boldness she had never imagined herself possessing, she crossed the final barrier of space that parted them and slid her arms around him, saying huskily, 'Forget about him and make love to me, Frazer. I've wanted you to so much.'

She felt him tremble at that last admission. His arms closed around her, his mouth brushing tender kisses along her jaw until he found her mouth, and then quite suddenly he wasn't tender any more, but fiercely passionate and demanding.

They undressed one another quickly and eagerly. Frazer paused to cherish the hard points of her breasts with kisses that quickly turned from adoration to desire, making her arch supplicatingly towards him, her quickened breathing impeded by her surprised sounds of pleasure.

Long before he laid her down on the comfortable bed, positioning himself above her and looking searchingly into her face, she was ready for him, rising eagerly to meet his first tentative thrust into her body, welcoming it with such heat and pleasure that his own caution deserted him and he cried out her name as desire quickened between them, bonding them like an unseen all-powerful current.

To sleep wrapped in the arms of the man one loved, protected by the bulk and warmth of his body, must surely be one of life's most special pleasures, Rebecca reflected drowsily, snuggling closer to him.

SHE WOKE UP FIRST, well before dawn, and, after the first realisation that it hadn't all been a dream, couldn't resist the temptation to reach out and touch him; at first simply to reassure herself that he was actually there and then later, because she couldn't resist the sensation of his skin beneath her fingertips, of his sleepy and yet total acceptance of her touch.

Lost in the new and proprietorial pleasure of investigating this territory that was now hers, she slid her hand to his waist and then lower.

'Can't a man get any sleep around here?' Frazer grumbled in her ear, but his hand was already trapping hers against his body, encouraging it in an exploration of intimacy that made her pulses race.

'Now see what you've done to me!' he complained teasingly against her ear.

But he didn't seem in the least displeased; far from it, Rebecca reflected dreamily as he drew her down against him and made tender lazy love to her with his hands and his mouth, arousing her so slowly and gradually that it wasn't until she started to tremble with the need to have him inside her that she realised the extent of his restraint and self-control.

Their lovemaking was intense and explosive, an almost violent unleashing of shared emotion and need that kept them locked in one another's arms long after their desire had climaxed.

'I hope I haven't made you pregnant,' Frazer murmured softly to her. 'Much as I want you to have my child, I need some time to have you to myself first. It isn't going to be easy,' he warned her. 'The twins...'

'Still resent me,' Rebecca said wryly. 'Yes, I know. But in time...'

'I can't send them away,' Frazer told her honestly. 'They're too young to understand.'

'I don't want you to,' she told him. 'They need you, Frazer. You're virtually all they have.'

He looked at her for a moment, then said softly, 'And *you're* all I want. All I've ever wanted. All I ever shall want.'

MAUD AYSGARTH heaved a sentimental sigh as she watched her nephew coming down the aisle with his bride.

Frazer and Rebecca, married at last! Thank goodness! A gleam of triumph lit her eyes. Of course, she had known years ago that they were meant for one another.

She was rather proud of the way she had engineered Rebecca's presence at Aysgarth. She blew her nose fiercely. Rebecca had never looked more beautiful. The way she was looking at Frazer, and the way he was looking back at her...

As the guests turned to file out of their pews and follow the bridal couple out into the unexpected warmth of the late September day, Maud felt a soft tug at her sleeve. She stopped and turned her head.

'Ah, Robert! How well you look, dear boy!'

Robert grinned at her.

'Never mind the compliments; just tell me one thing. How *did* you manage it?' He nodded in the direction of Frazer and Rebecca. 'How in the world did you get the two of them together when nothing that the rest of us tried could do it?'

Aunt Maud's Edwardian chest swelled, her countenance uncompromising and stern. 'Robert, I have no idea what you mean. Now, where is that lovely wife of yours...?'

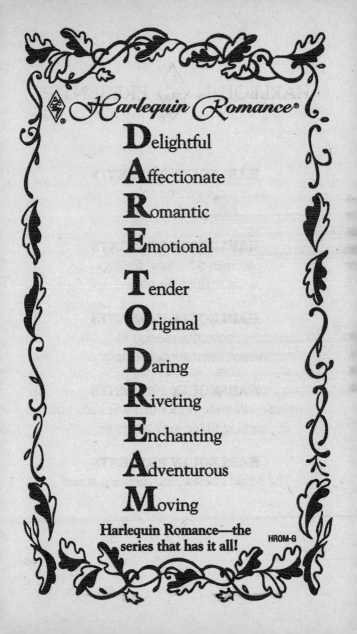

Harlequin Romance®

Delightful

Affectionate

Romantic

Emotional

Tender

Original

Daring

Riveting

Enchanting

Adventurous

Moving

Harlequin Romance—the
series that has it all!

HROM-G

HARLEQUIN PRESENTS®

HARLEQUIN PRESENTS
men you won't be able to resist
falling in love with...

HARLEQUIN PRESENTS
women who have feelings
just like your own...

HARLEQUIN PRESENTS
powerful passion in
exotic international settings...

HARLEQUIN PRESENTS
intense, dramatic stories that will keep you
turning to the very last page...

HARLEQUIN PRESENTS
The world's bestselling romance series!

Harlequin® Historical

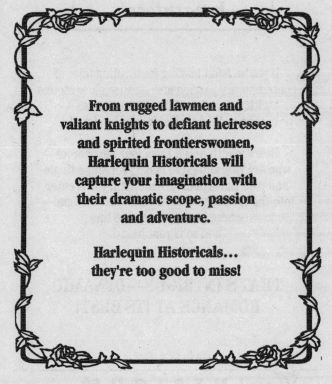

**From rugged lawmen and
valiant knights to defiant heiresses
and spirited frontierswomen,
Harlequin Historicals will
capture your imagination with
their dramatic scope, passion
and adventure.**

**Harlequin Historicals…
they're too good to miss!**

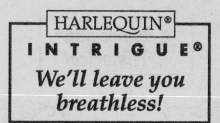

LOOK FOR OUR FOUR FABULOUS MEN!

Each month some of today's bestselling authors bring
four new fabulous men to Harlequin American Romance.
Whether they're rebel ranchers, millionaire power brokers
or sexy single dads, they're all gallant princes—and
they're all ready to sweep you into lighthearted fantasies
and contemporary fairy tales where anything is possible
and where all your dreams come true!

You don't even have to make a wish…
Harlequin American Romance will grant your every desire!

Look for Harlequin American Romance
wherever Harlequin books are sold!

HARLEQUIN SUPERROMANCE®

...there's more to the story!

Superromance. A *big* satisfying read about unforget-
table characters. Each month we offer
four very different stories that range from family
drama to adventure and mystery, from highly emotional stories to romantic comedies—and
much more! Stories about people you'll
believe in and care about. Stories too
compelling to put down....

Our authors are among today's *best* romance writ-
ers. You'll find familiar names and
talented newcomers. Many of them are
award winners—and you'll see why!

If you want the biggest and best
in romance fiction, you'll get it
from Superromance!

Available wherever Harlequin books are sold.

Look us up on-line at: http://www.romance.net